The Man on the
THIRD FLOOR

The Man on the
THIRD FLOOR

ANNE BERNAYS

The Permanent Press
Sag Harbor, NY 11963

For information, address:
The Permanent Press
4170 Noyac Road
Sag Harbor, NY 11963
www.thepermanentpress.com

Library of Congress Cataloging-in-Publication Data

Bernays, Anne–
    The man on the third floor / Anne Bernays.
        p. cm.
    ISBN 978-1-57962-285-5
        1. Book editors—New York (State)—New York—Fiction.
    2. Gay men—New York (State)—New York—Fiction.
    3. Homosexuality—History—20th century—Fiction.
    4. Upper East Side (New York, N.Y.)—Fiction. I. Title.

PS3552.E728M36 2012
813'.54—dc23   2012016407

Printed in the United States of America.

For Michael Korda, Ken Siman, and Michael Stein.

They have my back.

CHAPTER 1

After news of the unusual goings-on in my house finally escaped, like a gas leak from a faulty stove, some of my so-called liberal New York City friends characterized my life using words that shocked even me. "Deplorable," "disgusting," "unnatural," "selfish," "hedonistic," "bizarre." I hadn't hurt them in any way, hadn't threatened their way of life. Up until then we had had a lot of fun together.

Actually, this didn't happen. What did happen was that I was met with looks of incredulity fueled by moral judgment, averted eyes, hems and haws and, in some cases, total silence. I only imagined that they called me those things in the privacy of their own homes and to each other. "Can you believe it, good old Walter—all these years?" One or two of them, I guessed, were secretly envious because I had managed to fool everyone for quite a while and because they would have liked to do as I did but didn't have the nerve. The years when most of this occurred, a decade or more after the war ended, belonged in a time when there were more secrets held tight to the heart than there were gold-star mothers. In those days, not so long ago, men were supposed to cleave to their wives and women to their husbands. Any other combination was viewed as deviant. Psychologists listed these deviations in their diagnostic bibles under "sickness."

I wasn't sick and I wasn't angry. I was an easygoing person, someone who kept his temper in check and who listened to what other people told him without yawning or interrupting. I was told by several people that I exuded good will and prudence, and had decent judgment. The people I worked with at Griffin House liked and respected me, my children, Henry and Kate, seemed to enjoy my company; my wife, Phyllis, was attached to me—in her own way. She was an extremely attractive lady and her enthusiasms affected people like a virus. I had my share of enemies—what man doesn't, especially in a competitive atmosphere like book publishing?—but I know I was an okay guy, generous, flexible, known for my snappy joke-telling, especially during office Christmas parties. I picked up the check more often than not and put up with incompetence as just another little glitch along the way.

I also know that I didn't have the courage of a lion or a five-star general like Ike. I kept my public risk-taking to a minimum. The fact that, in Tolstoy's words, I eventually took on "the habit of passions" was a kind of fluke—I never set out to install a man on the top floor of my house and I kept these passions (actually I prefer the word "love") hidden from everyone except their object. I think if someone hates you they're probably doing so for the wrong reason.

⌗

I HAD a fairly easy time of it as a child, considering the disastrous histories of some families—drunkenness, battery, betrayal, absence, and all-round filthy behavior. If my father was off-limits emotionally and unable to empathize, and my mother not quite a whole person, I figure that's kind of par for the course at our stage of civilization. My mother, Belle Samson—born Gissler, and married at twenty—was a starchy type who couldn't quite get the hang of how to relax. She was devoted to my father, both sentimentally and as what they used to call a helpmeet. He came first, the children second. We were hardly neglected by if, say, she was reading to us and my father called out to her for something, she would stop reading. I had a younger sister, Constance, smart like me and chubby. When she was twelve she caught diphtheria and died three weeks later. This death virtually eradicated my mother's ability to laugh or smile for the rest of her life.

Belle was always persuaded that if God chose the Jews, he was partial to the German branch of this tree; she was something of a snob. My father, Maurice—Morrie to his friends, though not to his wife—the embodiment of Victorian rectitude and habits, died at the age of sixty-seven when he fell from the Super Chief and cracked his skull against the platform in Newton, Kansas. Maurice and his younger brother David ran Belcher's, founded by their father in the 1880s. This was a department store on lower Fifth Avenue and Nineteenth Street. Belcher's was the place women headed for whenever they needed curtains, cribs, napkins, kitchen gadgets, lamps, maids' uniforms, quilts, "notions," cutlery, dinner plates. In other words, the list of items you couldn't purchase at Belcher's was extremely short. Belcher's made Maurice Samson, née Shapiro, a rich man, and elevated him to that sector of New York society considered "privileged" and therefore obligated to donate money toward the health and security of the "underprivileged." My father could afford to send me to private school and summer camp, to enable me to move about more or less freely in New York living rooms not generally welcoming to the Jewish community. He was on the board of several charities and was a member of the Orange Club, an establishment that admitted only German Jews. He was considered a real gent. He wore spats, carried a Malacca cane, and called every man he met "sir."

When I was very young, my father raised his voice while talking to me as if I was deaf or a foreigner. It was very annoying. "Eat your vegetables," he would shout, "sit up straight." "Stop crying!" "Sportsmanship!" All of the instructions had a legitimate basis because I wasn't anything like the exemplary boy he wanted me to be. I was a crybaby; I was afraid of the dark, I wet my bed until I was almost ten. In spite of this, he was determined to instill the traits of manliness in me—sensing or seeing that this was an area that needed a lot of help—by demonstrating how to stand "like a man" with my hands in the pockets of my knickers and one leg thrown to the front and side, a sort of devil-may-care gesture.

He would have liked me to call other boys by their last names and give and receive noogies without a twinge. But instead of sneaking around with the boys to light up a forbidden cigarette, I preferred to read in my room: *Treasure Island*—"Them that die'll be the lucky ones," a sentence that scared me into imagining varieties of torture so awful they kept me awake at night, *Journey to the Center of the Earth*, *Tom Sawyer*, and an assortment of childhood classics. I loved to read *and* listen to music, Mozart, Bach, Debussy—especially Mozart, who seemed to be singing directly into my inner ear—and to walk around the city by myself. The mean kids in my class at school called me sissy because I was a clumsy athlete and because I just didn't seem to have the stuff of an all-American boy. That was okay with me; I figured it was better to be a sissy than a bully—I never fancied making people afraid of me. But all this was hard on father, who never stopped trying to make me into someone I clearly wasn't. My mother, who had a somewhat more generous nature, comforted me whenever she could, but she was afraid of my father's temper and hadn't the grit to defy him.

I promi̇ myself that if I ever had a son of my own, y the things to him that my father said to rned out to be a professional wrestler, or house, I'd keep my mouth shut and give

By the time I was thirteen or so, I had decided that it was easier to try to get along with my parents and especially my father, than to act sullen or provocative. I decided that I wouldn't reveal to them who I was or what I was thinking. I felt like an actor in my own play, taking the starring role and being the nice obedient child and young man they wanted me to be. It was hard at first, but I got adept at it and gradually my father stopped picking on me, though he never stopped asking me about which sports I was taking at school. He wanted it to be football but it was tennis and chess.

Camp Nayiwuk was nestled along the piney shore of New Hampshire's Lake Winnipesaukee, where it was so cold in August that ice formed on the top of your bucket of water overnight. I was a camper there for three years, starting when I was thirteen. I was by far the smartest kid at camp so that although I was no good at any sport but tennis (another fluke), the other boys left me pretty much alone. Intelligence will propel you far; but if you're born with an outsized I.Q., as I was, being smart is hardly different from having acute hearing or the sense of smell of a hound dog. It's just something you're born with, a gift from your parents that they didn't have much to do with. I was quicker than the other boys, the counselors, and even the head of the camp—a beefy man who had been a major in the First World War where his right hand had been blown off in the Battle of the Somme. We had to call him "Major," and whenever he forgot the name of a camper, he would lift his collar in back to read the name tape. Major blew the bugle to wake us up, summon us to the dining hall, which was half open to the elements, and send us off to bed. His taps was perfect. But he was not as smart as I was and never knew that I had brought an air rifle to camp, never knew that I walked off alone into the woods where I shot at rabbits and other small animals, never discovered that I got out of most athletic activities merely by walking away from the field. The others boys seemed to be afraid of my brain, which struck me as peculiar. What could I do to them? "Sticks and stones will break my bones but names will never hurt me." Most of them could have wrestled me to the mat in two seconds, but what could I do to them? Nevertheless, I was intimidating enough to keep them from beating me up. I had one special friend, Stanley Jacobs. Stanley and I would take long walks through the woods and talk about Herman Hesse, Thomas Mann, Stravinsky and other cultural icons. We must have been insufferable.

During my second year at camp I sprained my ankle tripping over a root; I wasn't the most graceful boy in the world. While the others kids worked up a sweat on the baseball diamond and basketball court, I lay on my bunk for five days reading the collected poems of Lord Byron. One afternoon during this vacation, Harmon Strout, a counselor, ducked into the tent I shared with three other boys. The counselors at Nayiwuk were clean-cut college students who needed school tuition money. Most of them had been there since the time they were campers; the place had about it an air of a grand secret society, with fire rites and pledges, and rituals. It was run with a strict autocratic hand that most of the boys found irresistible. Harmon was by far the most popular counselor at camp; he had a frankly Aryan glow, blond, tousled hair, bulging muscles and a touch of condescension that made you desperate to impress him. He could pitch a baseball clocked at eighty miles an hour, he was the fastest runner, he had earned every nature and boating badge. Most of the campers, especially the little boys, had crushes on Harmon.

Inside the tent, Harmon began to talk to me—something he had never done before; as a matter of fact, I was sure he was as oblivious of me as I was aware of him. And for me, it wasn't a physical thing; it was more like a mortal in the presence of a god. Harmon sat down opposite me, and looking into my eyes, told me he admired me. "You're one of the few brainy ones," he said. "And you go for nature. I like that." He inquired about my ankle. I made light of it. My heart was racing; I could feel my cheeks getting hot. Apollo was sitting on Dannie Nussbaum's bed. He told me he had almost flunked out of Bucknell but had managed to hold on. "I'm on probation," he said proudly. "I think you're my type." I didn't know what he meant. "I've brought some Vaseline," he said, digging into the pocket of his shorts and holding up a small jar for me to see. He stood up and slowly drew his polo shirt up over his head and out along his bronzed arms. I was having a hard time breathing as it dawned on me what he was up to. He stepped out of his white shorts; he wasn't wearing underpants. His penis looked huge and upright like the ones on Greek vases. I wanted to run away from him, I wanted to stay where I was. It was all happening slowly and fast at the same time, and I had the odd sensation that I was off to the side and above, watching. "I won't hurt your ankle, I promise," he said gently. "Turn over." I turned over and he pulled off my shorts. "Now turn on your side, away from me."

"Relax, kid," he said. "This is supposed to be fun." Then he instructed me—not in the tone he used while coaching tennis, but in a sweet whisper—what I was supposed to do. When his penis entered me I felt an electric shock so violent it made me scream. He told me "for crissake, be quiet." I held onto my voice as the shock melted and turned into a sensation of delight. I almost passed out. "There," he said finally. "That wasn't so bad, was it?" I couldn't talk. He put on his shirt and shorts. "Can't say anything? I couldn't my first time either."

"Harmon?"

"What is it, kid?"

"Nothing."

"Okay then. I want you to promise you're not going to tell anybody about what we just did. Not anybody, not even your best friend. You have to swear. Or I might have to hurt you."

"I swear," I said.

⚜

AFTER THIS experience I tried to bury my memory of it—the fear, the pain, and above all, the pleasure. I was afraid to tell anyone, and it didn't occur to me until much later that I could hardly have been the first, or last, object of Harman's affection—or whatever it was that brought him into my tent. I bring up this childish adventure mainly because it has some bearing on what eventually happened.

That morsel of luck, my swollen I.Q., got me into Harvard, a school with a quota system that counted Jews as if they were apples on the edge of rotting. At Harvard, I concentrated on Philology and minored in Psychology, a discipline that looked on the theories of Freud and Jung with an unhealthy skepticism. We learned mainly about the brain and its neurons and what makes monkeys different from men. No mention of the unconscious or, god forbid, the Oedipus complex or penis envy. I graduated from Harvard in '29, a memorable year to say the least. With money given me by my old man, I traveled a little, stopped in Paris for a while, got to know some people who later became famous, and realized that the thing I most wanted to do was to be involved in the publishing of books, and specifically, editing them. The creation of a book from the tiniest seed of an idea to the blossom you can hold in your hand seemed sacerdotal. It was a priestly calling. So when I got back to New York in '34, I applied and got, right off the bat, a job at Griffin House. Not incidentally, Griffin was owned by my mother's second cousin. I don't pretend to have the sort of personality that can walk in off the street and be immediately seated at a desk and given the services of a secretary. As a matter of fact, I was not seated at a desk, not for several years. I was sent on the road as a traveler, a somewhat fancier word for traveling salesman. The personnel director assured me that this was the way you put your feet on the first rungs of the ladder to publishing success. This meant reading the books on the list, getting to know the booksellers, being part of the process from idea to cash money. It wasn't easy—sleeping in crummy hotels, eating undistinguished food, being lonely—but in its own way it was satisfying, because I was learning the business from the business side, not the editorial side, where men made decisions based more on aesthetics than money. Actually, few people had the money to buy new books; books were a luxury, just as a car was, and a Harvard education. I would hang around in the little stores dotted here and there across the New England countryside and shoot the breeze with the employees who, most of the time, stood around reading the books they weren't selling.

So I had a good eight years at Griffin before I went off to enlist in the fight for Democracy. Meanwhile, I had met Phyllis Weiner at a party in the Village, a place I often went because I liked hanging around artists and writers more than the men I had gone to school with, most of whom had vanished into businesses or one of the weighty professions. I preferred to think of myself, while not creative in the conventional sense—I didn't paint, I didn't write, and I didn't make pots on wheels or take pictures of naked women in grayish light—I thought I understood why they did what they did (earning almost no money for their efforts). The party where I met Phyllis was given by one of the junior editors at Griffin House.

Jonathan Lehmann lived on the top floor of a house on Ninth Street between Fifth and Sixth; its rent was partly taken care of by his rich parents. Johnnie was someone endlessly attracted to new people and things, a collector of both. He was known for his parties and generosity with his liquor, just recently available again on the legal market.

Johnnie was, as my colleagues told me, "going places" on the strength of having recommended a book that made it on to *The New York Times* best-seller list, every publisher's dream. Phyllis was a copywriter at the advertising agency that produced the ads for Griffin's books. Having this job when most of her circle was having babies set her apart.

"Who's that girl?" I said.

"That's the infamous Phyllis Weiner," Johnnie said. "She writes copy for Hollis. Forget it. She has a boyfriend."

I was surprised, not that she had a boyfriend, but that Johnnie would assume that was why I'd asked, when I was simply struck by her style, a sort of Isadora Duncan gauziness when the prevailing style was sleek and satiny, Ginger Rogers as caryatid. Phyllis certainly stood out. Furthermore, she was smoking a cigarette in a holder that looked like ivory.

"Why infamous?"

"She leaves ripples behind her wherever she's been," Johnnie said. I asked him what caused the ripples. He couldn't or wouldn't supply any details. "Maybe it's just talk," he said. "Anyway, she's a looker isn't she?"

"Is she?" I said. "Doesn't she seem a bit theatrical?"

"Well, that's part of it," Johnnie said. "Excuse me. I think I see one of my celebrated authors . . ." And he was gone to greet a man with red hair whom I didn't recognize.

Phyllis saw me staring at her and gave me a look impossible to misinterpret. I was flattered, I have to admit. I also have to admit that although I hadn't been with any men since Harmon, my dealings with women were more casual than passionate. At least they knew I wasn't after "one thing." I liked women a lot; they seemed to me to have a core of good sense that most men didn't give them credit for. At this point I wasn't sure, really, what I wanted or needed. The idea of making love to a man ever again seemed as taboo as making love to a sheep. And I don't mean doing it; I mean just thinking about it. Terrifying. Making love to a woman, on the other hand, was okay, I had no trouble getting it up; but oh my god, how my mind traveled during the act. It went all over the place. The girl would be groaning and crying out—apparently I had something they liked a lot—calling my name and invoking the deity, and there I would be, lying over or under her and silently reciting lines from "The Waste Land": "He'll want to know what you done with that money he gave you/To get yourself some teeth."—a statement blunt and earthy and surrounded by a vision so bleak it made me shake all over when I first read the poem. Anyway, I had girlfriends and they seemed to like me well enough; there were several who not only hinted marriage but out-and-out asked me to marry them. One even told me "I want your baby." I demurred gracefully, telling them I was married to my work or some other bullshit. A couple of them cried; it made me feel bad, especially when they insisted that they wouldn't have gone out with me if they had known I was only "playing" with them.

Even at twenty-three, Phyllis was different. The look she gave me was a come-on, but when I did come on I found that she wasn't just a flirt; she had ambitions for herself that had nothing to do with babies—or even marriage. After we courted a while, Phyllis wisely restraining her more enthusiastic impulses and I trying to out-manly myself, we married in 1935 in her parents' apartment on Morningside Heights, went on a short honeymoon to Lake Tahoe, and then hurried back to our respective jobs. Phyllis was physically ardent and I did my best to satisfy her. It wasn't that I actively disliked sex; it was just that it seemed on the order of eating when you like the food well enough but you're not hungry, and your hostess is watching you so you eat it anyway.

We lived in a small apartment near Gramercy Park, a perfectly nice place with a living room flooded with light because of the empty lot next door. Phyllis was a copywriter but she didn't intend to stop there. She wanted to fix things, anything, even the design of kitchens—which she claimed had been done by men only, and men had no idea how high a sink should be or where to put the stove vis-à vis-the refrigerator, which she called the icebox. She wanted to fix society so that the Negroes didn't all have to live in only one part of town. She was almost in love with FDR, and if she heard anyone saying anything negative about him she would either engage that person in loud argument or, if she was tired, walk out of the room. To Phyllis, Roosevelt was a greater leader than Washington, more compassionate than Lincoln, wiser than Jefferson. Always a Democrat, I largely agreed with her and thought the New Deal a fine idea, with a few drawbacks, none of which I chose to discuss with Phyllis.

By this time I was back in New York—having finished my sentence as a traveler—and I have to admit, understanding a good deal more than I had when I set out, about why people bought certain books and left others on the bookstore shelf. I had done a fairly decent job and the higher-ups rewarded me by making me a junior editor, responsible both for "acquisitions" and for line editing. These two activities involve very different kinds of skills. For the first you need to make deals with agents, to feint and parry, to use exaggeration and hyperbole, even to lie a little to get what you're after. Agents are basically peddlers, depending on the fruits of others peoples' labor for their livelihood. On the other hand, agents, as the joke went, ought to be considered generous human beings because they give ninety percent of their earnings to their authors, keeping only ten percent for themselves. Line editing means having and employing the total focus of a good tough English teacher, dedicated to getting the words in the right relationship to each other. How many people possess both these skills? I suppose it would be immodest of me to say that I'm one of them, but what the hell. I enjoy the game-playing involved in acquiring manuscripts, and I love fooling around with words, trying to get them to say exactly what an author wanted them to say, not an approximation but a bull's-eye.

Meanwhile, Phyllis had left the ad agency. "Writing that stuff was cramping my style," she told me. "I want to do more of my own thinking, get involved with the real world." So she went and got herself hired by WNYC, the radio station started in the 1920s to focus on Manhattan and its boroughs. I considered myself a forward-looking man but I wasn't all that happy having her work; I guess it injured my pride. The wives of most of my friends stayed home and had babies or worked gratis for the Henry Street Settlement. If professional women weren't viewed exactly as freaks they were certainly looked upon with suspicion: why on earth would a women want to spend eight hours a day in an office when she could walk in Central Park, have lunch with her lady friends, go to a movie to watch Myrna Loy or Joan Crawford turn men inside out, stay in bed all day eating chocolates and reading *The Saturday Evening Post*? We hired a nanny, a French woman named Michelle, who insisted on being called "Mademoiselle." She looked after our two children—Henry born in '38, and Kate, in '41— while Phyllis plied her trade. At first I felt bad about leaving them in the care of a gray-haired mother substitute, but the children hung on to her and gave her kisses so I figured she must be okay.

Then Hitler invaded the Sudetenland after promising he wouldn't, and in the words of John Milton, all hell broke loose. Phyllis joined the Red Cross. They sold her a snappy uniform and visored cap and she rolled bandages. During the second year of the war, I told Phyllis I was thinking of enlisting.

"They won't take you," she said. "You're too old."

"Thirty-five isn't old. I'm just a pup."

"What would you do? You hate guns."

I realized I hadn't told her about the air rifle that was now broken down and stashed away on a shelf in the hall closet. "Nothing with guns," I said. "They'll find something for me to do."

And they did. Largely I think because of my Harvard Education, they found a place for me in army intelligence, gave me a set of lieutenant's bars, and set me to work along with fifty or so other young men, passing on more or less routine decoded German messages. This meant reading hundreds of them a day and seeing to it that they got into the right hands. It should have been more exciting than it turned out to be because a lot of the messages were about supplies of milk for the troops, some weather reports (which we already knew), and the deteriorating condition of some of the tanks on the North African front—sand in the gears. We were all housed in one large room in the recently completed five-sided building out of which the war was conducted—in the strategic sense. My job wasn't anything like my peacetime work at Griffin House except that they both dealt with words.

After a certain amount of good-natured grumbling, Phyllis joined me with our children: Henry, then a serious-minded four, and Kate, a one-year-old, whose face made me weep it was so beautiful. Mademoiselle, meanwhile, had gone to work for Sikorsky on Long Island where she made three times the money she had working for us. Phyllis hadn't wanted to leave New York, because that was where all her friends lived and she was working on being a recognized "hostess." I teased her about this, telling her that the mayor's address book didn't have as many names in it as hers did. Moving to D.C. meant having to make new friends to invite to small, candlelit gatherings in our Georgetown apartment, a place we rented for the duration at an exorbitant price. After a couple of weeks Phyllis was, basically, a good sport about it, finding a nearby kindergarten for Henry and wheeling Kate around in our pre-war English baby carriage. She had wonderful posture and stood as straight as Mary Poppins.

I enjoyed wartime Washington. The odor of power floated, cloudlike, above the city, penetrating ceilings, walls, bedrooms. It amazed me to see how easily men wielded it, instructing other men (and some women) what to do without please or thank you attached. Just do it and do it now! This was something I had never been eager to do. For instance, whenever I needed something typed up or mailed or delivered down the hall I said, "Would you mind please doing so and so"—as if they had a choice. I don't know why I was so bad at giving orders. Maybe it was because my father was a boss of the old school and never softened a command. And the odd thing was, the people who worked for him in our house didn't seem to mind his brusque Prussian style. What was the matter with them? Could they actually enjoy being foot soldiers in my father's army? In any case, Washington agreed with me and me with it, even though Phyllis missed New York, and I had no guarantee that my job at Griffin would be waiting for me when the war was over.

After a month or so I began to be aware that I was being stared at. Whenever I glanced in the direction of the gaze I saw a man who looked somewhat younger than me. A man with intense gray eyes, an expression of curiosity and a snappy haircut. I was uncomfortable being stared at, and just as I made up my mind to walk over to him and ask him what the hell he was doing, the watcher himself approached me and stuck out his hand. He introduced himself as Edgar Fleming, following this with "You're in publishing, aren't you? I mean when you're not here fighting this fucking war."

I asked him how he had found this out, wondering at the same time what he was up to. I especially didn't want to think about him sexually; I was over that, had been for a long time and considered the incident at camp a childish experiment, not worth dwelling on. Fleming told me that he

21

thought I looked "interesting" and had asked about me. I told him I'd been only a junior editor, low on the ladder.

"And I'm only a junior writer," he said. "I've published a couple of short stories. One in *Collier's*."

If he was telling the truth then he really was a writer. While no *Hound and Horn*—rarified, often experimental— *Collier's* published stories by Hemingway and Faulkner. I felt like a fisherman who discovers that the river is full of trout. I looked at Fleming's face; it had the right amount of gloom plus something else, an element that suggested profundity that doesn't necessarily have to deliver. He would look just fine on the back of a book jacket.

It didn't take long before Fleming admitted that he had written a novel. He followed this by the inevitable question: Would I read it? Of course I would read it. What did I have to lose? If I liked it, I would send it along to the editor-in-chief at Griffin, Fred Forstman. This would, at the very least, show Forstman that even while I was working away to help end the war my heart still lay in my peacetime job. If I thought the manuscript was no good, I might risk our new friendship; this was a risk I was willing to take. I called Phyllis and told her not to wait for me for dinner, and asked Fleming if he'd like to go out for a drink after work. We went to a place in Georgetown crowded with men in uniform and others who looked as if they had been recruited from the life of the professions and business to work for the government. They were making a good deal of noise and there was the kind of laughter that's just a little too loud. We found a table just then being vacated by a gray-haired Colonel and a young girl, probably his secretary, whom he meant to bed after filling her with an expensive dinner. As they headed toward the door, his hand caressed her right buttock.

During the next hour or so and two whiskey sours each I found out that Edgar Fleming had been born in a small town in California, where his parents still lived, had gone to

U.C.L.A., had worked for General Motors writing in-house advertising copy and was not married, not yet ready to "settle down." I put this inside quotation marks because he tended to use tired phrases when speaking, a habit I hoped hadn't spilled over into his written prose. I wasn't surprised when Fleming told me he was single: he had made himself famous by working his way through almost the entire cadre of secretaries who worked in our top secret department. Apparently he had the touch that combines the neediness of a boy with the emotional muscles of a "real man." He seemed to be irresistible to women. Our waitress called him "honey" while twinkling her tired eyes at him.

Fleming brought his manuscript to work the following day. He had packed it away neatly in a typewriter paper box. "Here's my baby," he said.

I told him I would read it as soon as I could. And then I asked him to promise that if I didn't think it publishable, he wouldn't let it destroy our friendship. Even as I said this I was aware that the friendship, like newly poured cement, had not hardened enough to last if something came along to put a big footprint in it. I knew that if I said no the friendship would evanesce. At the very least he would not only take my rejection as a personal affront but would probably write me off as a moron. Does a couple whose marriage has shattered actually believe they can remain friends?

The manuscript was over six hundred pages long. First novelists generally were long-winded as if the stuff had been building up for years, until it finally erupted and spewed great flows of words and ideas. The most egregious example of this was poor Thomas Wolfe who, in his first novel, disgorged thousands of pages, leaving his editor to take up (changing metaphors) his machete and whack away at the words until they could fit inside the covers of a book it didn't take a muscleman to lift.

It wasn't all that easy to read at home. Home was the

third floor of a house owned by a couple in their seventies who probably made a mistake renting to a family with a toddler (Kate) and a four-year-old (Henry); but, as they told us, they felt they should be doing something toward the war effort and so had made the top floor—which had previously housed their children—available to a serviceman and his family. Phyllis spent a lot of time telling Henry to be quiet and rocking Kate so she wouldn't cry. I didn't have a study; I worked at the table where we took our meals. It was cramped, and although I enjoyed hearing the happy—and sometimes not so happy—noises made by my children, I found it hard to focus on anything other than my surroundings. But when I started reading Edgar Fleming's manuscript I was stuck to the chair, so to speak. It was a Saturday morning and Phyllis had taken the children to play in a nearby park. It wasn't until they came back to the apartment that I came out of my trance, as I heard them making their way up the steep staircase, Kate crying, probably hungry, and Phyllis, being mother hen. Henry burst into the room and ran over for a hug, which I gave him, only half aware of what I was doing.

Fleming had managed to keep his story of war in the Pacific moving ahead at a steady clip while not neglecting to flesh out his characters, one in particular who I figured was self-referential, a good guy with a touch of uncertainty who comes through in the clutch. Happily, Fleming had avoided clichés and manipulated his characters through assorted problems like a pro. The hand-to-hand scenes were especially dramatic, not to say lurid, and at one point I had to put down the page I was reading because I was too moved to read further. Adding richness and nuance to this recipe, he had delivered a story that was fresh and surprising. Fleming was one in thousands. I'd been in the business long enough to know the astronomical odds against getting a first novel published. You don't want to think about it if you're writing one. I'd say the odds were less favorable than playing the French horn in the New York Philharmonic. I spent the rest of the day thinking about Fleming's novel. One more thing—and this is an editor's most reliable gauge for judging a novel—I forgot that I should have been using my most critical eye, and instead I fell into the delighted reader category.

The thing held up very well, right to the final sentence on the last page. Fleming was a thoroughbred. Aside from solidifying our friendship, he and his book would help secure my place at Griffin. I would back the right horse. This horse, a rarity, had both literary lines and the potential to fill the coffers of Griffin House. Not too many like him—Pearl Buck, John Steinbeck, Somerset Maugham, Daphne du Maurier—came to mind. I thought I was way ahead of my new author, having immediately started complicated calculations. If I allowed my enthusiasm to shine too brightly, Fleming might then get an agent who would sell his book to the highest bidder. Griffin House, though one of the three clearly "Jewish" publishing houses, was not famous for its generosity to authors. It wouldn't have the fight to compete with, say, Harper Brothers or Macmillan.

I figured that it wouldn't hurt Fleming to cool his heels while building up a pool of self-doubt, and so I waited until he asked me if I had read the manuscript. "Well," he said, Have you read it? What do you think?"

I told him I'd finished it the night before and that "there might be something here. Yes, I definitely think you've got something here. Of course it needs a good deal of editing and cutting. But I'd like to pass it along to our top editor, Fred Forstman. See what he thinks."

"You really like it?" Fleming's eyes glittered and widened.

"Yes," I said. "It moves right along. Strong characters, good plot. I can't say how Forstman will respond but he usually likes what I like." This last phrase was pure imagination; Forstman and I had not had that much intercourse, so to speak. "I assume you've got a carbon?"

"No. Should I have?"

This was a trusting soul. One of Hemingway's wives had left a suitcase on a train filled with the only copy of her husband's novel, still in manuscript. When he found out what she had done I could imagine the rage simmering, then boiling over, ending with a stinging slap to the cheek or, better yet, since Hemingway fancied himself something of a boxer, a perfectly executed right to the jaw. But why had the novelist entrusted his only copy to his wife in the first place? Was he hoping something like this would happen so he would have an excuse for sloughing her off? I'd read just enough Freud to grasp the notion that there are no accidents. Or was the missus envious of Ernest's gifts and celebrity and so purposely left the suitcase on the overhead rack before leaving the train? Or did she, smarting from the inattention of a husband more occupied with his work than with his wife's soul and body, want to punish him by leaving his work on the train? I believe their marriage went up in flames shortly after this sad event.

I told Fleming that he would have to get one of the department's stenographers to copy the manuscript on her own time. "You'll be lucky if you can get it done for two bits a page."

He balked, saying he couldn't afford it. "You watch," he said. "I'll get it done for nothing."

Damned if he didn't. It took her three weeks, and she did a first-rate job: very few obvious erasures, only one or two typos. I asked him what he would have done had something happened to the manuscript. Fleming, flipping through the copy, said offhandedly, "I'd sit down and write it again. Sure I could. It's all here inside." And he tapped his head with his forefinger.

I wrapped the manuscript myself in the mail room and

took it to the local post office where I sent it off to Fred Forstman first class. I taped a letter to Forstman to the outside of the package, a letter I rewrote three times in an effort to tiptoe successfully through a transaction that could turn out badly if I wasn't extremely careful. If, for example, I sounded too enthusiastic, Forstman, a small person—no more than five-foot-eight and all shaky ego—guarded his territory like a toothy animal bred to frighten off intruders, if not actually bite them. Almost anyone seemed like a marauder to Forstman. To say he was reluctant to share credit is putting it mildly. He had been known to reject a manuscript solely because he believed the editor who recommended it was getting too big for his boots. With this in mind I played down my role in the discovery of this rare talent named Fleming. My letter read, in part: "This manuscript is the work of a man in my department. He seems to be fairly well in control of the material and keeps the reader in mind most of the time, an admirable trait as you well know, especially in a first novel. While there are soft spots (see especially the scene in the mess hall when a nurse breaks down—too drawn out, not altogether plausible) and an occasional lapse in logic and coherence, Fleming manages to keep several balls in the air at the same time. While no O'Hara or Steinbeck, he does merit, I think, a second look. He came to me, I didn't go after him; and I have to admit to reading the last half faster than I would have liked. . . ." This was a lie, designed to show Forstman that I was capable of a little too much haste. "The novel needs a whiz-bang title of course, to help move it along. Have we seen a war-in-the-Pacific novel? I don't think so. On the other hand, there might be several of them out there waiting to get published. This may add up to a great big nothing, but as you yourself always say, you don't lose anything by another read."

CHAPTER 2

Day thirteen came and went without a response from Fred Forstman. It was ridiculous, I knew, to be so invested in the outcome, but somehow I had got Fleming's future and my own confounded so that the outcome grew in importance the longer I waited to hear from him. He couldn't not like Fleming's novel; it was too obviously the real thing—nothing but truth in it. A moron could have recognized its quality.

I had always thought of time as moving right along while we humans stood still, grabbing at it, as if it were a string being pulled too rapidly in front of us by an invisible hand. But now it went by too slowly, barely moving. On day fourteen I said fuck it, and decided to phone Forstman. I was about to dial when the boy from the mail room dropped the morning's mail on my desk. The Griffin logo—an implausible creature with an eagle's head and wings and the body of a lion, and what that had to do with publishing books, who knew?—was visible from several feet away. I felt like a high school senior hearing from the Harvard admissions people. I tore open the envelope. I needn't have worried. "A winner," Forstman wrote. "A page-turner. Couldn't put it down; Judy had to literally pry it from my hands so I could get some sleep." He assumed I knew that Judy was his wife. I was relieved, though not surprised by his response.

This man had started out as the manager of a company that mass-produced bread in Queens, and by some circuitous route no one could describe, landed in the sales department of Griffin House in its early days, gradually working his way up to editor-in-chief. He had also bought into the company to the tune of forty-nine percent. The other fifty-one was owned by the publisher, making him the principal owner. The publisher, a man whose way I tried to keep out of as much as possible, had no literary pretensions, but he did own the place and one was smart to keep that in mind.

Forstman set his own style in the office. From my small but probably accurate sampling, men at the top of their profession didn't play by the same rules ordinary workers did. They used foul language freely and often to make their point. Some of them shouted when miffed. They came and went at will any time of the night or day. Fred Forstman, for instance, often spent the night on his office couch. He was expansive when pleased and told stories about World War II and his part in it, how he dabbled in the black market selling gun parts and other assorted military leftovers. It didn't seem to make any difference that his stories were a mix of fact and fantasy. The turnover of his secretaries was legendary; some of us kept score. Once in a while one of them could be seen weeping in the hall outside his office door. I assumed he had given them a pinch on the bottom. There was a lot of this kind of thing going on at Griffin House. I walked in to the production department one day to check on a jacket design and found a new young secretary sitting on the art director's lap. Neither seemed the least bit embarrassed.

Forstman was known around the office as a cliché expert, like the one in *The New Yorker*. His memos, riddled with them, were passed around by his staff, for laughs, like dirty limericks. But he had a kind of idiot savant's nose for which book, still in manuscript, would turn out to be a commercial success. If, additionally, the book also drew the admiration of critics from, say *The New York Times* or *The*

Saturday Review of Literature (in my view hopelessly middle-brow, but never mind), so much the better. But commerce was far more to Forstman than what, with a faint sneer, he labeled "belles lettres." You couldn't send your boy to Yale with the proceeds from the sale of belles lettres no matter how many awards they won. To show he understood his younger and more idealistic editors—and to prove he was no troglodyte—Forstman made sure some of our more rarified and hard-to-sell products were placed alongside the blockbusters in backlit nooks in the reception area.

Once in a great while, maybe every five years or so, a book would straddle the chasm between moneymaker—the kind of book people read on the subway—and the achingly truthful, profoundly revealing, luminous, unforgettable work of fiction by Evelyn Waugh or Edith Wharton, for example. But the appearance of such a book was almost as rare as the legendary green flash.

In the end, of course, Forstman took entire credit for the birth of a major new American voice, the first writer to chronicle—with soul-searching truth and gritty realism—the bloody battle against our enemy in the Pacific theater in a novel entitled *Men at Sea, Men at War*. Buoyed by a generous advertising budget, the book took off like one of the V-12 rockets the Germans started lobbing over cities in England near the end of the war. *Men at Sea* also accomplished that rare chasm-straddling maneuver, earning nods of approval from reviewers and critics who mattered, as well as from composers of college syllabuses and conveners of conferences on "the state of the novel in a changing world" and similar head-scratching topics. Meanwhile, it secured a place on *The New York Times* best-seller list for six months.

Fleming began to feel the heat generated by the flames of publicity. He was flooded by requests for newspaper and radio interviews. Agents sent him letters asking to let them represent him, girls who had seen his photograph on the book jacket wrote him, suggesting the two of them meet and submitting names of hotels in the City. Movie producers from the West Coast called Griffin's rights and permissions department to see if they could buy the rights to his story. *Look* magazine ran a feature about him, with pictures of the man of the hour with his parents, and with a Hollywood starlet. He seemed mainly amused by this attention but, basically, untouched by the dust kicked up by his novel; it didn't go to his head. I was delighted about this and when I asked him about it he said, "I have to be thinking about the next one." I could have told him that if you hit it big with a first novel, the reviewers are out for your scalp when number two comes out.

A few weeks after his novel was published Fleming said, "Don't you think I ought to get an agent?"

"Oh, I don't know, I suppose so. But you're doing great without one. If you get one you'll have to turn over ten percent of everything you earn to him."

"It might be worth it," Fleming said. We were having a drink in a bar filled with men in uniform and obvious government workers who had loosened their ties–literally and metaphorically—and were trying to flush the tensions of the war out of their systems with strong spirits. Fleming motioned to the bartender to bring us another round. "Then I wouldn't have to think about the financial stuff. I do the writing, he does the figures. Isn't that the way it goes?"

"Who've you been talking to?"

"Nobody in particular," he said. He still wore that starry-eyed look, as if he'd bent over to pick up something sparkling on the sidewalk and found it was a diamond brooch.

"Listen, Ed, I'm going to level with you. Of course you need an agent. All writers need an agent. They do your dirty work for you. I'm going to help you get a good one. But if you ever breathe a word of this to Forstman or anyone who might tell him, it'll be curtains for my career. Well, maybe not curtains, but it certainly won't send my stock soaring with the boss."

"I don't get it, but I'll agree. I don't understand what all the fuss is about."

"The fuss is that Forstman believes he'd be much richer if it weren't for those pesky agents—and he's probably right."

I knew I was stepping a little out of line in helping him sleep with the enemy. But Fleming was my friend. We liked each other. We trusted each other. Why not give him an assist?

So I helped Fleming find an agent, John Bailey, a small gesture of friend to friend. Bailey was a legendary shark admired by writers, feared by publishers. All I had to do, really, was make a telephone call to Bailey. When Forstman did discover who was representing his newest and brightest author, he made some remark about how fast Fleming seemed to be wising up.

Fleming came over to our apartment for dinner at least once every week. Phyllis liked him to the point of flirting with him and vice versa, but never seriously enough to make trouble. Little things, like his praising her ingenuity in turning one small chunk of meat and a chicken neck into a delicious meal for five.

One night, after Fleming had been over for dinner, Phyllis said, "You know, one sign that Edgar's really okay is that the kids like him. I think children can tell whether or not someone's genuine."

This was one of those sayings that emerge easily and that I'm somewhat skeptical of. Does it mean that children can spot a phony more accurately than an adult? And if so, why should this be? Kids have limited intelligence, limited judgment. Anyway, I kept these thoughts to myself and agreed that Kate and Henry seemed to like listening to Fleming's jokes and his stories about what it was like to grow up next to a California bean field and what it was like (heavily edited, of course) to be in the wartime navy.

"And that's why," Phyllis said, "I find it so odd that he's a Republican. Aren't most writers Democrats?"

"I don't know. I guess so." For so long everyone had been focused exclusively on winning the war and their political opinions lay more or less dormant. Everyone pulling together, all eyes and hearts on one goal, differences buried. Now that the war was almost over, small fault lines had begun to appear and groups of this or that, some to the right, some to the left, were making noises. I have to admit that I had heard Fleming voice opinions about the Russians that surprised me and that I didn't share. Phyllis loathed this kind of attitude. She wasn't a Communist, she had never even considered joining the Party (as some of her dopey friends had), but she sympathized with their basic urgency to narrow or close the gap between those who own and those who merely work. She was, as I've mentioned, a liberal Democrat down to her toes.

"I don't know any Republicans," she said, as she went off to take a shower before getting into bed.

"Well you do now," I said. "I'm not going to change my mind about him just because he voted for Wilkie. He's a good guy—even the kids like him. You said so yourself."

"It's just strange he thinks those things. He hates the Russkies more than the Krauts. Jesus!"

⁂

AN ATOM bomb, something none of us had ever heard of—although there had been rumors during the war about a miracle weapon that could destroy a city in a flash—fell on two Japanese cities. The war ended within days. The bomb was so shocking that most of us couldn't manage to consider its implications and so ingested its reality whole, thinking about it in its narrowest terms, as just another weapon in the armory. After V-J Day there was general rejoicing, and for weeks people went around in the kind of euphoria usually associated with strong drink or drugs. We gradually cooled down and went back to the life we once had led. Only after we left our apartment in Georgetown and got back to New York did I discover that I didn't have my Benny Goodman and Artie Shaw records or my Victor recording of Mozart's *Requiem*. When I wrote our landlady she denied any knowledge of them, and I knew she had simply declared them a dividend for having to put up with two small children.

Our apartment was on Eighty-Seventh Street between Second and Third Avenues. It was in an okay building with a costumed doorman and an elevator man named Max who knew everybody's business. Your mail was delivered on the floor right outside your door. The place was small; my mother would have called it a matchbox: Kate and Henry shared a room, an arrangement neither of them would have chosen, a living room and a dining room so tiny that when you pushed your chair back to get up it hit the wall behind, leaving a mark. Post-war life seemed to flow more or less seamlessly from pre-war, the interruption better forgotten than dwelled upon.

Henry got his first pair of eyeglasses at the age of eight; they made him look owlish and didn't help with his popularity at school. He told me he wanted to go to Harvard, like me, precocious child. Henry seemed preoccupied with the war and kept asking me what being a spy was like. I told him I hadn't been a spy even though the work I had done was classified. "I never got overseas," I said. He seemed disappointed. He wanted to know if Hitler was really and truly dead and I assured him he was. Would he grow up to be a nervous Nellie? Kate, at six, had the kind of face photographers love: large blue eyes, and an expression that suggests premature cognition: *I know what you're thinking. I know how things work. I know how to make a perfect omelet.*

As for Phyllis, nothing much had changed since the first year of our marriage. She had always kept a part of herself off limits to me—not the sexual, but the opposite, the parts lying deeper beneath the surface. I'm not talking about her dreams or the girlish secrets she shared with her best friend, but intentions, shades of meaning, bits of family history, apprehensions. On the other hand, she was extremely vocal with opinions that had no immediate impact on either of us, especially about politics. Her sympathies clearly lay with those she felt had drawn a lousy hand in the game of life, so to speak. She was adamant about Truman, maintaining that he shouldn't have dropped the A-bomb.

"Yes, but it saved an awful lot of American lives. It ended the war," I said.

"I know. American lives. But what about all those Japanese lives? Don't they matter?"

Whenever I tried to engage her in conversation about things she considered trivial, such as whether Randolph Scott was a fairy or Sinclair Lewis was a genuinely classy writer, she got a jelled look on her face that said, "Let's get this over with." But how can I be sure that I interpreted that look correctly? She reminded me a little bit of May Welland in Wharton's novel, whose "abysmal purity" left her husband Newland in the emotional dust. Of course, May wasn't volatile, just steely. But she and Phyllis could have been sisters as far as their convictions went. Like May, Phyllis never did anything overtly awful or destructive, but she had placed a boulder between us that I couldn't budge. After a while I guess I gave up trying. But at least I had Henry and Kate, who were openly affectionate and were always asking me to take them to Central Park and buy them ice cream on a stick.

The war ended in August. I went back to work at Griffin House in September. They had given my old office to a lady editor who smiled at me in a friendly way as I walked down the hall. They had to scramble to find me another place for my desk, my shelves, my files. My new office had a window that looked out over Madison Avenue. I figured that Edgar Fleming had something to do with my new digs; he had upped my status with the house. The manuscript of his second novel, *Clarion Call*, a bildungsroman about a boy with just a bit too much curiosity growing up in rural California, had recently been edited, copy edited and sent to the production department, where they had farmed out the jacket art to a hotshot designer. Meanwhile, the promotion and advertising people were gathering to plan a campaign to put the novel over via fireworks and searchlights. Hollywood was sniffing around, having been alerted by Forstman that the new Fleming would be an ideal vehicle in which to insert Glenn Ford or Jimmy Stewart before stepping on the gas pedal and driving swiftly to the bank.

After a couple of months, Forstman—spurred, I imagine, by a touch of retroactive patriotism—announced in a memo to the staff that henceforth Walter Samson, "who did not have to go off to war but volunteered, temporarily putting his career at Griffin House on hold," would bear the title of senior editor. It was about time! I was given my own secretary, a small but noticeable raise, and new status with the serfs. All this was gratifying, to say the least, and I congratulated myself on being able to let my boss take the credit for MY discovery. Fleming was one of the golden geese of Griffin House, along with a book on soup cookery and the memoirs of a famous heavyweight boxer, ghost-written by a sixty-year-old grandmother, a real pro, who had also written the autobiographies of a polar explorer and a French resistance fighter.

Family life began to seem like the only life. My mother came to dinner every Tuesday, bringing with her gifts for the children, carefully chosen, prettily wrapped, a book or a pair of angora mittens or a wallet. She and I got along fairly well. This may have been because we were pretty formal with each other; I kept most of what I was thinking to myself and I suspect she did the same. My mother and Phyllis circled each other like two wary dogs. I don't suppose any woman adores the girl who marries her son, but I never once heard her say anything sharp to my wife—even though her eyes may have said the opposite. I was gratified by what I seemed able to take from a privileged life, but the usual feelings of "isn't there anymore?" would strike me from time to time, usually around three in the morning, and I would have to rebuke myself: you want too much.

Along about this time, Phyllis began a campaign to move the family to a larger apartment or, preferably, a house. This wasn't like her; although she dressed like a diva, she often bought her clothes at thrift shops on Third Avenue where, she said, you could find the most amazing castoffs. She didn't care about the kinds of things that brought a lot of women an access of pleasure along with a sense of superiority, like luggage from Mark Cross (now that people were allowed to travel abroad again), expensive clothes for the children, crystal chandeliers, modern furniture from Sweden, Georg Jensen silver on the table. So I wondered what was going on. I asked her outright.

"You're a senior editor at a major publishing house," she said. "But we live like you work in the mail room."

"You're exaggerating," I said.

"Well, I probably am. But you know what I mean. Just look at the dining room wall."

Phyllis and I actually shared the same relatively simple taste in most things. I never bought a lot of expensive clothes—though I did get my suits at J. Press because they made sure of the fit. I didn't especially like fancy cooking or glitzy parties and, above all, I enjoyed solitude and never felt that being alone was a lonely thing.

Phyllis reminded me that my father had left me a "fortune," a word that made me squirm; I preferred a euphemism like "a good deal of money." "We can afford a bigger place," she said. "I'd like the children to have their own rooms. They would too."

It would have been silly of me to resist what was an obvious choice; besides, I had no good argument with which to counter her proposal.

So out she went, with a real estate agent whom she referred to as "Sally" after their first meeting. Together Phyllis and Sally toured houses on the Upper East Side (having together decided that an apartment was not what the Samson family was looking for). Phyllis didn't ask me to look at any of them until she was pretty sure she had found what she wanted. It was a house on Eighty-Ninth Street between Park and Third on the downtown side of the street. It was a block or two uptown of what was considered the most desirable real estate in the city and, for that reason, Sally assured us, "the price is right." In other words, it was somewhat less costly than a house say, on Seventy-Fourth Street. These are the kinds of nice distinctions that mattered to Sally. I could tell, by looking at Phyllis' eyes, that she thought this part of the adventure was silly. But we were happy enough to pay what we did. It was a hell of a lot of money but we had a lot of money. "This is an investment," Sally kept telling us.

"I wish she'd shut up," Phyllis said about Sally. "She's making it harder for me to say yes. Whenever I'm pushed I back off."

But Sally kept pushing and, really, the house had everything to recommend it. It was just sitting and waiting for the Samson family. It was a four-storey brownstone whose front steps had been slashed off to meet someone's aesthetic standard, the stoop having been seen as a holdover from an another era and thus awkward. So you entered by going down three steps into what was originally the basement, and climbed up through the insides of the house along a narrow but graceful staircase. The kitchen and dining room were on the bottom level. Next floor up, the living room and a library I used as my study. The previous owners had installed floor-to-ceiling bookshelves in the library, which made me want to live in this house. Climbing rather steeply, you reached the third floor where the bedrooms were: Phyllis' and mine in front, with windows looking out over the quiet street with its spindly little trees favored by dogs on leashes, and two smaller bedrooms in back for the children. Still higher, half a storey, were several maids' rooms, and it was in one of these that my life swelled with secret pleasures. Kudos to Phyllis for insisting we move to a larger place; she had no idea, of course, that her urgency would change my life forever.

❦

MY GENERATION—I was born in 1908—had our heads turned by the idea that the United States was a melting pot. (Read some of Henry James' non-fiction for a contrary view. He considered non-English-speaking immigrants who crowded New York and a few other large cities as riffraff. He was a snob and I'm not.) My parents didn't want to be seen as anything but true-blue Americans. We German Jews considered ourselves to run right down the middle of the mainstream of American life, pulled along by the same currents as were the old Dutch and English families. Still, we didn't kid ourselves that everyone who was securely attached to high society would treat us the way we would like them to—with hugs and kisses. There was a lot of Henry James under the water—as well as on the surface. Harvard, when I enrolled, had a quota for Jewish boys that kept our number down to something under five percent. Only the Jewish boys and their families noticed; everyone else failed to notice—or if they did, figured it was okay. You didn't want too many of these smart but funny-looking youths filling the seats in Sever Hall.

But while I couldn't have passed through the front doors of the Union League Club without meeting the frozen gaze of a human barrier wearing a uniform and asking, "Excuse me, sir, are you a member?" I did belong to the Orange Club. Phyllis made fun of me for belonging and almost never went there with me. But I did like it. This institution, housed in a Florentine structure a few feet east of Fifth Avenue, was the equal in elegance and tone to any exclusive social gathering place in the city. You have to be a member of a posh club to appreciate its seductive appeal and the absence of even the remotest possibility of abrasion caused by a social mis-understanding. A private club may be anathema to people like Phyllis, but they do offer the same kind of emotional bonding that summer camp does. The Orange Club's grand, curling staircase with crimson carpeting anchored at every step by a stout brass rod, formed a pathway between foyer and second floor which was entirely dedicated to eating in a cavernous dining hall. Here, widely spaced linen-draped tables stood beneath the dead gaze of bison and elk, few of which any member had ever seen, much less slaughtered, outside a zoo. The Orange Club exuded the hush, odorless wonder of money and power.

I confess to having enjoyed myself at the Orange Club without too much guilt about the plight of most of the world's population. You can't feel guilty all the time. I often invited authors and agents to have lunch with me there. After we took our place at the table, a well-trained waiter would hand them a menu printed on heavy stock. "I never knew a place like this existed," I heard more than once, meaning, I guess, that they were surprised to discover that not all Jews ate hot pretzels and franks peddled from a cart on the sidewalk. I tried to convince Phyllis that the Orange Club represented not ostentation but its opposite, as there was nothing vulgar or in questionable taste inside the walls. Only conservatism, everything muted, subtle, the money things cost hidden beneath the ease and quiet, including the fact that you never heard a door bang shut, the clatter of dishes or cutlery; you never heard a burst of loud laughter.

⸾

LOOKING BEHIND me, I'm especially aware of just how chancy it was meeting Barry Rogers. It reminds me of the Thomas Hardy poem about the Titanic and the iceberg. Hardy, of course, believed in fate, believed that the convergence of these twain as he called them, had something of the supernatural about it, the gods were cooking something up for the ship, if not for the iceberg. When you make a connection that could happen only once, that connection takes on an extra significance that you can call anything you want—accident, coincidence, fate.

I sat in my office one afternoon reading a manuscript sent me by one of the most senior agents, a man who represented H. G. Wells, Somerset Maugham, John Steinbeck, and Daphne du Maurier. He was known to have the most productive and lucrative stable in the business, which meant that when one of his submissions arrived by messenger, you dropped everything to read it. It did not mean, however, that everything he sent over was publishable. This manuscript was crammed with stale ideas, equally stale characters, and an exotic setting about as convincing as the backdrop of jungle in a sixth-grade play. The author was a celebrated storyteller, so I could only conclude that this was something that had been moldering in a bottom drawer of his desk for years.

Someone knocked on the door. I was delighted by the interruption. I told whoever it was to come in.

A young man, I guessed to be twenty-seven or eight, entered briskly. I noticed his face first. He had the look of a swarthy angel, radiating beauty like that of an Italian noble in a Renaissance portrait. His mouth was full and slightly crooked. His eyes were dark, almost black—they shone as if polished. My heart beat rapidly and my chest tightened. I couldn't tell what was going on except that I knew I was looking at this man as if he were a woman.

"What can I do for you?" I said. He was wearing dark blue pants, thick-soled shoes, and a thin Eisenhower jacket. He carried a clipboard and pencil.

"I'm supposed to measure your room for a new carpet."

"Really?" I said. "No one told me."

He consulted his clipboard. "You're Mr. Samson?"

"That's what they tell me."

"This won't take more than a few minutes," he said. "I'll try not to disturb you."

Disturb me? He had disturbed me profoundly. I nodded, meaning nothing, temporizing. I pretended to go back to the manuscript, trying desperately to shake off the effect created by the man's bent back and powerful legs.

"What's your name?" I said. I hadn't meant to say this out loud but apparently I had because he said "Barry."

"Barry?"

"Barry Rogers." He took from his jacket pocket a large object which turned out to house a length of metal measuring tape on a reel.

I looked again at his black hair, beaky nose and olive skin. There was no way he was Rogers. But this was America, the land of altered names. If he was aware of my staring at him, Barry Rogers did not let on as he measured, wrote, measured again, wrote again, bending, straightening, doing a dance around the room, in fact humming very softly to himself. My reactions to this Figaro suddenly reminded me of Harmon Strout, and what we had done at summer camp came out of my memory's hospital room, revived, and sent dangerous warmth through my body. Thank god I was sitting. Bits of thought presented themselves, one of them being that somewhere deep there lurked a Walter Samson who might want to be loved by a man more than by a woman. At the same time I dismissed this notion; how could that be true when I was married, had children, and considered my life a model of productive domesticity?

Was Barry homosexual? Did he know what was going on?

"I'm just about done," he said, standing up straight and stowing the tape measure in his pocket. He walked over to the window. "Nice view you've got here," he said. Still he made no movement toward the door.

"I like it," I said, swallowing hard. "Who did you say you work for?"

"Winchester Carpets," he said. "We do mostly commercial jobs. They all want wall-to-wall these days. If you ask me, I like to see some wood flooring with some nice polish. It's classier than a rug. But I probably shouldn't be saying this."

I nodded, partly because I agreed with him and partly because I couldn't trust myself to speak without sounding like I was strangling. What Barry was saying was banal, but to my ears at that moment it was like the prose in the King James version of the Bible. For a second, we looked straight into each other's eyes. Then we both looked down, gripped by caution.

"Well, I'll be going now," Barry said. "I'm supposed to be doing Mr. Forstman's room next. He gets the best grade of carpeting we turn out."

"Oh?"

With that stinging remark, the lovely young man turned and headed for the door. My chest tightened. I couldn't bear the thought that I might never see him again. I coughed.

"Did you say something?"

"No. But I was thinking. No, never mind."

"No," he said, "You did say something."

"I was wondering if you would like to meet me for a drink later, after work—if you're free of course." Truly, I hadn't meant to say this; the invitation came out involuntarily, like a hiccup. Something I had no control over was drawing me into something that might be risky. My life had been wrinkle-free up until now, a private education, Harvard, a wartime job that kept me on native soil, and a good job in a so-called gentlemen's profession. Whatever I knew about risk remained largely in my imagination. And now, standing not ten feet from me was a layer of carpets (though he probably didn't do the actual hammering) who threatened to change the shape and dimensions of my comfortable existence.

"Sure," he said. "That'd be okay I guess." He was casual enough, as if he'd been expecting this invitation from the moment he looked at me sitting behind my white collar desk. I covered my pleasure at his answer and suggested we meet at an out-of-the-way place I sometimes stopped in at after work for a solitary whiskey before heading home to wife and children.

Barry said he would meet me at about a quarter to six. "Your name's Samson, right? Like in the Bible?"

"Samson like in the Bible," I said. "See you in a while." I looked at my watch. It was just before three. How could I stand to wait for three hours before seeing him again? I couldn't work for the rest of the afternoon because I was so scared that he would change his mind and fail to show up.

CHAPTER 3

I t was several weeks before I told Barry my real name, and when I did he said that he too was traveling through this life under an alias. "It's the American way, right?" he said. "Like John Garfield, like Kirk Douglas." He was talking about two movie stars who had transmuted their Jewish-sounding names into something much more American. The war may have taken care of Hitler but anti-Semitism still lingered, like the bad breath of a person with the flu. "Give us a kiss, Shapiro," he said to me, "and stop looking so worried. What have you got to be so worried about?" Barry had grown far more familiar with me since our first meeting over a carpet, having assumed a kind of cheeky attitude which I three-quarters liked; the rest made me a little nervous.

"That carpet charade wasn't really you," I said.

"Sure it was, it was my job. I did a good job."

"But it wasn't really you."

"Just another side of me," he said. "We all have a lot of sides. Even you. Especially you." And he gave one of his melting looks that touched me so deeply I felt my cheeks go hot.

By this time Barry was fully inserted into our *ménage*—now *à trois*. Phyllis had no inkling of its true nature. After I persuaded Barry to move in with us—and it didn't take much persuasion as he was living in a crummy room at the Y and hated it—I had to tackle Phyllis' justifiable reluctance. My imagination went into overdrive: I told her that Barry had been a driver overseas during the war and added—not true—that he had been Omar Bradley's personal driver for six months. "You couldn't ask for better than that," I said.

"But Walt, we don't even own a car. We don't need a car. We take cabs. Why am I telling you this? You know this. I don't understand . . ."

She had a point. And editors in publishing houses didn't generally get driven around town by chauffeurs; they took the bus or the subway or walked just like all the other working stiffs. But I had enough money from my dead father, and I fancied the notion of being alone with Barry at least once a day—although we probably could do no more than look at each other in a meaningful way. I scrambled: "I saw a Mercury today in that showroom on Park; it would suit us very well. It's nothing fancy, not like a Lincoln or a Cadillac, but it's a sturdy car and, oh, I don't know, it would be nice to have our own vehicle."

"Stop! It doesn't matter what kind of *vehicle* it is."

"It's dark red, sort of muted crimson. You'll like it, Phyll. I sat in the backseat—it's very comfortable."

I told her we wouldn't ask Barry to wear a uniform. Maybe a cap. He was down on his luck, living at the Y, a war hero, if one insisted. The lies came so easily. I told her Barry barely made minimum wage from his carpet job. And most of that went to his old crippled mother who lived in Queens. "He's a good egg. I sort of feel we owe it to veterans to give them a break."

Phyllis' ears pricked up and she asked me just how much I knew about Barry.

"Not that much," I said. "Actually, I'm not sure how I know even this much."

Phyllis was less hard to persuade than I would have predicted. But I wasn't going to waste time trying to figure out why. "You'll be glad in the end," I said. I gave her a hug.

I got a kick out of making up stories like the one about Omar Bradley, one of my heroes. Sometimes I thought I had more imagination than some of my authors, who struggled so mightily to keep their readers from hearing the gears of a plot grinding its way through the pages of a book. I suppose I ought to have felt somewhat guilty and maybe I did—who wants to admit to lying?—but after all, I assure myself, who was it hurting? Not Phyllis, not Barry, not me. Certainly not the real hero—General Omar Bradley.

We were at the dinner table drinking coffee out of demitasse cups. It was nicely bitter. The children had asked to be excused to go upstairs to do their homework. It was one of those suspended moments at the end of a day, things having been accomplished, nothing much left to do. I had a manuscript to read waiting for me on my desk in the library but, having glanced through the first chapter at work, I knew I could dispense with it easily. (Pity, too, because it was a book about communications in general and television in particular, a baby that had just been born; most people couldn't afford a set but I had a feeling it was something that might seduce a good many readers away from books.) The trouble with this manuscript was that the author couldn't write and that's a drawback for someone who wants to publish.

"I guess there's plenty Barry can do around the house," Phyllis said. "When he's not ferrying you or me around town. He can shovel snow and wash the windows—inside. He can polish the banisters. Oh, and my mother's silver." As more tasks sprang up, Barry began to seem indispensable. "Yes," she said, taking her napkin off her lap and laying it next to her demitasse cup. "Are you sure we have the money?"

The room upstairs was empty. He wasn't going to eat that much. Besides, I was a clever investor and trusted the stock market to keep me in Mark Cross tan kid gloves.

❧

FRED FORSTMAN's health began to go downhill at about this time. He coughed a lot and seemed tired. The skin on his cheeks turned from ruddy to wan. He didn't talk about this but everyone noticed. There was whispering. The spring had gone out of his step, his loud voice grew hushed. It wasn't wrong of me, was it, to try and figure out who would succeed him? I'm certain I wasn't the only one to engage in this kind of speculation. The poor guy wasn't even sixty-five but it was obvious that he would—absent a miracle—be forced to retire sooner rather than later. Over the past month or so Forstman invited me several times to have lunch with him at the Orange Club, where he insisted on talking about the book business. He asked me to sit in on meetings with the heads of the advertising and promotion departments, and to come along when he met with agents of significance and the chief honcho of the Book of the Month Club. I felt these were definite signs I was next in line to the throne upon which sat the editor-in-chief of Griffin House. There was just one fly in the soup. Forstman had gone the same route with my pal, Charlie McCann. We compared notes and joked about the openness with which Forstman seemed to be pitting us against each other. Forstman, his eyes narrowed and carrying the trace of a mean little smile, was enjoying his game so much that it wouldn't have been a leap to infer that not only was he enjoying it, but might also enjoy watching us—me and Charlie—begin to hate each other. Unfortunately for him and fortunately for us, nothing like that occurred.

As I get older, I'm more and more aware of the pleasures of friendship and of the price you pay if and when it breaks apart—who cares what the reasons are? A broken friendship leaves a nasty scab. In any case, Charlie and I were pals, as I said. But where I greeted each new challenge with a spurt of adrenalin and a couple of sleepless nights, Charlie walked ahead into the unknown or the challenging with remarkable calm. He had spent several nights in the waters of the South Pacific after his destroyer was torpedoed by the Japanese, bobbing around in a life jacket, convinced he was going to die wet. This experience left him with a stoical view of everything around him, sparing him the usual ups and downs. Nothing was either very up or very down for Charlie but rather a kind of straight line, his graph not dramatic but, in the end, saving him much grief—and its opposite, much joy. Charlie would express genuine detachment where other men might have raged.

Charlie and I had both entered publishing as trainees before the war, and after it was over, climbed on parallel ladders, our feet on parallel rungs. It was eerie the way we were in lockstep. Each of us made senior editor in the same year, each had brought in so-called literary fiction and non-fiction as well as the more valued best-selling novels with breadth and sweep, guns going off, women giving birth without anesthesia, fast cars, millionaires, forbidden love, miscegenation, bloodshed, and emotional turmoil in bucketsful. Sometimes I had to hold my nose while editing one of these babies, while yearning for the purifying, sinus-clearing prose of Joseph Conrad or the sinewy language of Hemingway. But the blockbusters were, in the words of Fred Forstman, our "bread and butter." For the less commercial fare, I followed their progress through production, promotion and advertising—if there was any—very carefully, and tried to keep their authors happy under trying circumstances. "Why don't you run an ad for my book?" "How come [slot in author's name] got interviewed by the *Times* and I didn't?" "Aren't you going to send me to Chicago?" These poor guys didn't realize that in the book biz it's a Darwinian world, a microcosm of surviving if you're very fit. And the fittest books had the most money behind them. I could make a keen argument that without these Griffin House would have failed and closed up shop. For every ten dollars we spent promoting and advertising one of our commercial items, we spent twenty-five cents on a delicate, mid-list novel whose author was lucky if his book didn't end up on the remainder table within six months or else shredded into bus transfers.

When it was clear that Fred Forstman could no longer escape the consequences of cancer, when he could no longer walk up a short flight of stairs, he sent a memo to the entire management staff announcing his plans to retire the very next week. No one was surprised by the memo. In fact, they were surprised that it had taken so long. There was a subdued party at Louis XIV at which Forstman was given a Cartier watch. The watch was not my choice; why would a dying man want to be reminded of the passage of time? Forstman seemed pleased in spite of what could have been an awkward moment; he accepted the gift with a sad smile and a lame joke about not having to floss anymore. He was sixty-four and a lifelong smoker of Camels.

After the party broke up, I suggested to Charlie that we go have a drink at Clarke's establishment. "Was that a wake or what?" he said.

After we settled ourselves at a small table in the back room, I said it right out: "I'll be your pal whichever of us gets the job."

"Ditto," Charlie said. "I promise that if it's you I won't shoot myself. I like what I do. It suits me fine. I know I should want to climb up a little further but, you see, I don't actually care that much. Of course I care but not that much. The other day I got a manuscript about a chimpanzee who plays chess. It had possibilities. I see illustrations. What do you think?"

"I think you're pulling my leg." The two of us were getting sloshed.

"Okay, maybe," he said. "But what I mean is if one of us gets the job, the other won't get it. One winner, one loser. Am I not correct in that thinking?"

"Definitely," I said, hearing my words blur. It sounded like I said *definulty.* "What I want to know is if you're not going to shoot yourself, who are you going to shoot? Me?"

"Absolutely! I mean absolutely not! You're my buddy, my ole buddy."

"I lost out on the Mailer," I said gloomily.

"I lost out on the Shaw," he said. "We're even. More money, that's what. Fucking Boston tight-asses. We're even tighter than they are."

I told him they hoarded their money, then spent it all in one lavish gesture. I had wanted the Mailer—almost as much as I wanted to see Barry when I got home each night. We didn't talk for a while. Someone we both knew slightly from another house came over to the table and asked us if it was true about Forstman. Both of us told him we didn't know what he was talking about. I began to wonder whether Phyllis was getting ticked off because, as my watch indicated, it was almost six-thirty. I really wanted to see Barry and my kids. "I gotta go," I said, getting up and realizing that I was not all that steady. "I'm going to take a cab home. Can I drop you?"

Charlie declined, saying he thought he'd better walk.

❧

THE NEXT morning I arrived at work headachy and dry-mouthed, carrying my attaché case, unopened since the day before. As I lay it down on my desk I saw a note asking me to go see Forstman as soon as I got in. A sliver of joy struck the back of my neck and traveled down my spine. Until this happened I hadn't allowed myself to count on this promotion. As I knocked on the door to Forstman's office, I realized that sweat was dripping down my flanks.

Forstman's voice had lost its timbre but you could still sense the energy that had worked for him for years. He was assuming I knew why he had asked me to come see him.

"You want to know what tipped the scales for you?" he said. Without waiting for an answer he said that it was my work in intelligence during the war. "Nothing to do with your work here." That was heartening. "You and Charlie, I could have flipped a coin. I figured any man who can go into the service and emerge with his balls intact has got what it takes to do this job. I mean deal with lunatic authors and greedy agents and the rest of the pack, especially those fucking show-off reviewers who think we give a hoot about how much they remember from graduate school. I want to know for crissake whether I should read the effing book, not whether he can recite the poems of Christopher Smart." It was Forstman's style to trash everyone he happily did business with. I reminded him that Charlie had been in the navy. "It's not the same thing," he said, shaking his head. "Not the same thing at all." I really didn't know what the difference was, just that he had chosen me and not Charlie for whatever reasons he had constructed. Did it matter?

I was ecstatic for twenty-four hours. Then my concern for Charlie kicked in. Even Barry's kisses and endearments failed at first to make me feel better. "Do you think Charlie'd be moping around if he got the job instead of you? You're acting like a girl!" I thought that was pretty funny, considering what we were doing at the time. I guess I brightened up a little. I knew I was being stupid about it, but I couldn't help putting myself in Charlie's place and I knew how much it would hurt me. Sissy boy. I shook my head to get rid of the blazing face of my father that had appeared suddenly on my interior horizon, telling me to be a man.

The following day I insisted that Charlie allow me to take him to lunch, a gesture that could have been read as a symbol of my newly acquired power. Charlie one-upped me by ordering a split of champagne and as it bubbled away in its flute, Charlie wished me continued good fortune and good health. "And while I'm at it, good luck to Ike—these are weird times. Who's to say who's American and who isn't? Why do we have to prove anything?"

There was not even a token argument about who was picking up the check. "For Pete's sake," Charlie said, "Don't look so glum. You're right where you want to be. God help you if something bad happens. . . ."

"You're right," I said.

"Shit, man, Charlie said, "It's only some lousy under-paid job. There'll be more headaches for you and more sleeping with lady authors for me. You know I get all the lady authors."

I looked at him sharply.

"Just kidding," Charlie said. "There was only that one time—and it was her idea." He wouldn't tell me who it was.

I stepped so easily into Forstman's shoes that I was hardly aware of a breaking-in period. Fairly soon it was obvious to me that what he had done as editor-in-chief was not all that different from my own work, except that he got paid a lot more for it than I did. I told Phyllis that I seemed to have been born for the job. My wife, whose father was a celebrated professor of English and rhetoric at City College, smiled in that superior way of hers, no doubt assuming that in sensitivity, taste, judgment, book-learning, and all-round literary sensibility her father was light-years ahead of her husband even if he did have an important job in pub-lishing. Did I mention that she had a definite thing about her father?

When we were first married I was annoyed when, from time to time, probably when I was at my most vulnerable, she compared me to "the Prof," as she referred to Daddy. But I had grown used to it; it seemed to be an autonomic reaction. Also, in about the same marital era, we had come to a kind of sickish understanding—her idea—which was that nothing counted if it was not said aloud. This included body language, smirk, eye-roll, frown, abrupt turning away— none of these counted as genuine messages. So her superior smile talked to me, unheard but not unfelt.

By this time, Barry Rogers had lived in my house on Eighty-Ninth Street for about a year serving as driver, handyman, occasional butler (although he chafed at having to wear a dinner jacket and black socks and shoes, and accused me of taking advantage of his good nature). I tried to see him alone at least once a day but this wasn't always possible. Kate was seven, Henry was ten, and they were always running from one room to another. I had taken over the library for my study. I retreated there after dinner several times a week, mostly reading manuscripts or scribbling odd ideas on a legal pad. Sometimes Barry would meet me there for a swift kiss and a few loving words and a joke or two but it wasn't safe; we both knew how risky this was but we did it anyway.

I was constantly amazed by how profoundly Barry's presence in my house affected me, especially on those days when our paths did not cross. I was happy just knowing that he was walking in the same space I was or applying Butcher's wax to the banisters, polishing the silver, or having a smoke in the servants' tiny dining room off the kitchen with its one dusty window giving out on a still dustier air shaft. Or maybe lying on his delightful back reading one more book about fly-fishing, or tinkering with the beautifully engineered motor of our car, which he kept waxed and buffed to a fare-thee-well. The car lived in a garage a few blocks away in a reserved space I considered outrageously expensive. Barry had a strong attachment to the car, which he called Baby, not an original name but you couldn't joke with him about the car; it really was his baby. All day long, while performing as loving husband and family man, as decision-maker, as shaper of the reading public's taste, while talking on the phone to a tearful author or editing yet another Edgar Fleming sure-fire best seller, or sharing some in-house gossip with Charlie McCann, while listening gravely to the head of production, a whiz (though completely nuts) named Oliver, I longed to hold Barry and have Barry hold me, naked, vulnerable, exploring each other in the silence of passion and contentment. I never questioned my choice of lover—it was simply a fact accompanied by a breathtaking risk of the forbidden.

Each night when I got home I knew that Barry would be somewhere in the house, waiting for me. "Good evening, Mr. Samson, sir. I trust you had a pleasant day." He would lay it on, the formality. "Yes thank you, Barry. Is Mrs. Samson home? The children?" Our eyes darted quickly over each other's features in a gesture of deep devotion and play. Did I feel the sting of guilt? Not at all. For I told myself I wasn't hurting anyone, but never considered that if my game was discovered, my marriage would collapse and god only knew what else would happen to me; I was breaking all the rules of conventional society and many people could get justifiably indignant.

After being greeted by Barry, who took my topcoat and hat, I would spend the next hour or so having a nice quiet cocktail with my wife, while letting my mind wander all over the place. Kate and Henry would join us for dinner where Phyllis made certain that events then current would be brought up and discussed. Phyllis was especially vocal on the subject of Israel. Her father had always been fervidly anti-Zionist. She said, "Just watch, it will end badly. You just can't plunk down a state where there are people already living and tell them to go find someplace else to live. Just like those poor South Pacific Indians or whatever they were when we tested the atom bomb. Just leave, get off your island! They had no choice." Kate and Henry could be articulate enough—both their schools made them learn poetry and then recite it in front of the class—but when their mother hopped astride one of her hobby horses they wisely held back. No one could ever accuse Phyllis of being a shrinking violet.

From the outside we were a handsome, loving family. And we were! I swear we were. The wife an unconventional beauty, the children bright-eyed and endowed with energetic curiosity. Few could have guessed that Kate, with her straight blond hair and turned-up nose, had Jewish parents. This made it easier for her to navigate through a world in which anti-Semitism had a foothold, not that she was in danger of being hauled off in the middle of the night and never heard from again. Henry, on the other hand, had thick dark curly hair, a large nose and pools of gray grief beneath his eyes—all of which were likely to tip people off as to his Hebrew origins and slam the door hard. But he was extremely bright; I figured he would go into something like theoretical physics, where he would excel. I wasn't really worried about him. Most of the men who worked on the atom bomb were Jews, their origins conveniently overlooked because America's life was at stake.

This business about being Jewish in a largely Protestant environment was one I preferred not to bring up more than was absolutely necessary. After all, the Samson family was secular—we didn't go to temple, we didn't observe the holidays or holy days, my children were generally ignorant on this subject. But one night Kate asked why the Jews had not accepted Jesus as the messiah. (I suspect they were singing Handel's oratorio at school.) And I said, somewhat flippantly, that maybe Jesus just wasn't messiah material. And she said, "Well, an awful lot of people think he was."

I didn't have a clue as to how to proceed with this subject so I let it drop, though Henry and Kate exchanged glances I read as being not entirely favorable. The problem was too large, too complicated. At least we weren't Negro. Every few months you read in the newspaper about another lynching in Alabama or Mississippi, the poor man strung up by a mob of redneck morons and left swinging in the breeze, eyes open and turned to a delinquent deity.

⤳

THERE WAS one nagging problem and I was smart enough not to blame it on anyone but myself. And if I'd been that sort of man—as so many of my colleagues apparently were—I would have found myself on an analyst's couch complaining that I couldn't talk on Sundays. I can just hear him say, "What does the word Sunday suggest to you?" "Well I don't know, really. Day of rest? You know I'm Jewish?" He makes a "yes" sound. "So that means my Sabbath is on Saturday, not Sunday." "Everyone else's Sabbath is on Sunday so the difference is only nominal." Was I here to hold a theoretical discussion or was I here to fix what was broken? "I try but it's as if I had something stuck way down in my throat." "Tears?" "Of course not! Why would I be crying?"

So I was a mess on Sundays. At the time, I wasn't inclined to do much soul-searching, or trying to figure out what was going on; I was juggling just about all the balls I could handle. If forced to say why I turned into a mute every seventh day, I would probably suggest that I was only truly at ease at work, and in the embrace of my sweet Barry. (Well, he wasn't all that sweet, but rather that combination of sweet and peppery the best cooks turn to when they want not only a distinctive but a memorable flavor.) Sundays were a palpable domestic reminder that I was living a life of secrets and shames. This, as much as anything, closed my throat and stopped my tongue.

Phyllis managed to busy herself or go to the movies with one of her friends, or in several other ways ignored me because she knew perfectly well that nothing would bring me out of my funk. I mostly stayed at home and wandered around the house like a wraith. In 1949, Kate was seven and Henry, ten. Sometimes they would try to tease me into playing a game with them. They loved Monopoly and played for hours on the Persian carpet in the living room. I heard them shouting and tried to avoid being spotted, but Kate saw me and cried, "He's got both of them, Dad; he's got Boardwalk *and* Park Place."

"I bought them fair and square," Henry said, trying to engage my eyes with his.

"He always gets both of them," Kate said. "It's not fair!" Kate's eyes grew wide, produced tears, and sent them down her lovely cheeks. With a sudden motion, she lifted one side of the board and tilted it high so that houses, hotels, cardboard deeds, variously colored paper money, and game pieces went sliding down over her brother's knees. Henry looked at them in disgust, as if they were cockroaches.

"It's not fair, Dad," Kate said again, her voice ragged with pain.

Henry and I stared at each other, abashed, as if it were us and not Kate who had done something startling and shameful. Then Henry said, "I'm not going to play with her anymore. She's just a baby, a crybaby. She knows I got them by paying for them! That *is* fair."

I wanted to negotiate. Henry was technically right; Kate, younger, more vulnerable, and not yet resigned to the way things worked in adult-land, had a point. He did get the best properties every time. Why? It would have been nice to get down on the floor with them and try to navigate through this maze. Instead, I patted Kate on the head and left the room. I guess I wasn't the best father in the world, but at least I cared.

One Sunday in October, Phyllis had persuaded her younger sister Vera, who lived in Purchase and often filled in when Phyllis was busy, to take Kate to see *National Velvet*, her favorite movie. She had already seen it a couple of times and had, as far as I could tell, a full-blown crush on Elizabeth Taylor, in every way Kate's opposite. Henry was in his room with the door closed, no doubt studying, something he was extremely skilled at. Young scholar, surely headed for M.I.T. Phyllis, who had just recovered from the flu, was taking a nap; her post-sickness naps usually lasted an hour or more. I took a chance and began to tiptoe up to Barry's room on the floor half a storey above ours. Barry had gone to visit his mother in Queens, who had made it known to him that she expected to see him on her door-step every Sunday—except, of course, if his job interfered. Okay, so he was a dutiful son; I was the neglected lover. I couldn't help smiling about the role I had opted for. It was ridiculous, as silly as if I had volunteered to be a tree in a children's play. And still I couldn't help feeling that he had stolen our time together and did not care as much as I did. He held me in a suspension of doubt for which I had absolutely no grounds. This is how far I had veered away from the routes shown on every civilized map.

I reached the top step only a little out of breath. The air here was different, musky and smelling like wet rags. Before the war, four or possibly five servants lived in the rooms, but since we'd owned the house, first just Grete the cook and Marie the housemaid occupied them. Then Barry came, making three in all. The others had been converted to storerooms or were simply left vacant and undusted. The hallway, painted tan, was lighted with a couple of sixty-watt bulbs hanging on chains from the ceiling. In each cell there was a sink attached to the wall, with separate spigots for hot and cold water, a small desk and chair. A skinny bed set against the wall, and a very small armchair with a padded seat. Some of the windows looked out over backyards, ours and our neighbors', and the others on an air shaft. When Barry first saw his room he said, "Well, it certainly ain't the Ritz." I reminded him he was getting it for nothing, and he said, "Not exactly for nothing." There he was, putting me on the debit side again.

But I didn't care; he was the deepest, most satisfying love of my life, and though I knew it couldn't possibly last,

I did my best to tamp down the doubts in order to savor what I held tightly in my grasp.

All three rooms were empty because Sunday was a day off for everyone. I slipped into Barry's room and closed the door quietly behind me. The room smelled sharply of its occupant, that Kreml hair tonic he overused on his black hair, and something else tingly I couldn't identify, maybe toothpaste, the remains of which stuck in a pink blob on the edge of the sink. I looked around, not sure what I wanted to find, for, in spite of Barry's assurances and caresses there lurked this fear that someday he would tire of me and simply take off. Did I find signs of betrayal? Restlessness (as evidenced by a map or a guidebook to the Italian Lakes)? A burgeoning bad habit (drugs? booze?). There were no obvious hiding places in this sad little room and I saw the usual items: several books on fly-fishing piled up on the floor, this odd taste having no outlet so far as I could tell, a Whitman's Sampler half-full, a pre-war Philco radio he had forgotten to turn off emitting swing music, Benny Goodman I think. I knelt and buried my face in his pillow, feeling sorry for myself for things that were, basically, trivial, not worth dwelling on. The world had very nearly blown apart, the war's effects lingering still in what some considered a very lucky conclusion. If it had not been for finding the Enigma code machine or the atom bomb, our part of the world would be cracking rocks in Georgia. I had no call to feel rotten simply because my lover had to sleep in a room unworthy of him, and because, in spite of the pleasures it afforded me, my double life required more emotional stamina than I wished to expend.

It wasn't easy, after all, keeping a lover under the eaves like a poor orphan while my wife and children occupied the rest of the house in style and comfort. It wouldn't be unreasonable to wonder why I didn't, at this point, take off and leave with Barry. I thought of it many times; Barry and I talked about it. Something kept me from changing the pattern of my life. It wasn't just one thing, it was a cluster of them, made up in part by my job, which I loved, my family, especially my children, my own history of caution, the formidable voice of my father prodding me along narrow and straight paths, always maintaining the best posture. All of these formed a tight impenetrable ring around me, holding me firmly inside. If you question why Newland Archer didn't leave the "abysmally pure" May Welland for juicy, sophisticated Ellen Olenska—I'm thinking about *The Age of Innocence* again, and how well Edith Wharton could write about inertia without losing the pace of her story—you come up with the same conclusion about Newland that you might have about me: neither of us were brave enough to rock the boat. Some of my earthier mates would substitute "balls" for bravery.

Phyllis barely tolerated servants in the house, although I could get her to admit to liking the concrete results of their presence. "Buzz, buzz, buzz," she said. "They're worse than mosquitoes." My view is that, being the daughter of an academic father and a musical stay-at-home mother, she was uncomfortable being waited on. She was not a princess. She preferred doing things for herself, and she made the children straighten their rooms and put their soiled clothes in the hamper, scrub the ring from the tub, and never leave towels on the floor. Shortly after we bought the house I persuaded Phyllis to hire Grete to cook our meals (Phyllis didn't like to cook and as a result was a poor one). Marie, the maid, came somewhat later when Phyllis discovered dust balls beneath the sofas and chairs in the living room and study, and Grete wouldn't clean anything except the kitchen table and her precious knives, insisting that was not what she was hired for.

I admired Phyllis' independence of mind and refusal to let our money make her lazy, but there were several things about her that got under my skin, like having opinions with a capital O. Once started on a charged topic, like the Taft-Hartley Act, and she had something to say about it—in this case that it was "evil"—she had a difficult time letting it go. Dog with bone on which strands of meat still cling. Kate would roll her eyes at me—"There she goes again"—but wisely keep her pretty little mouth shut.

Getting to my feet, I took one last look around Barry's room. A damp towel lay on the floor under the sink. I picked it up and stuffed it into the space between the rod and the wall, noticing as I did this that the wall was streaked with tears of rain leaking through cracks in the ceiling.

I checked my watch, having lost track of time. Phyllis might be awake and wondering where I was. I was sure she didn't suspect what was going on or, if she had suspicions, she kept them buried so far beneath the surface that even she would have a hard time recognizing what they were. I walked softly back downstairs to where Phyllis and I shared a wide bed. I squared my shoulders and opened the door softly. Phyllis was lying on top of the spread with a light blanket drawn up just past her waist. Her eyes were closed and one plump arm lay on top of my pillow. A sudden pang of love—not desire—sprang up inside me. This middle-aged woman, the mother of my children, had a good heart; what had she done to earn a scamp like me? She opened her eyes and smiled at me. "What time is it?"

"It's almost three," I said.

"I was testing to see if you'd answer."

I asked her what she meant.

"I mean you never talk to me on Sundays. You never talk to anyone." Phyllis raised herself on an elbow. One of her large, dangly breasts revealed itself over the edge of her robe. Her aureole was a target, the nipple a bull's-eye. "Your vow of silence on Sundays. You're a monk."

"That's nonsense," I said. "You don't know what you're talking about. I'm talking now, aren't I?"

"For a change," she said. She got out of bed, pulling her robe tightly around her. "Would you like to go for a walk in the park," she said. "It's one of those good October days. And I feel much better."

I told her I was glad she felt better and sorry that I couldn't go for a walk; I had a lot of work to finish.

"Well, then," she said, "I think I'll go by myself," and she trotted off to her dressing room closet. "I need some fresh air."

I could have gone with her. I don't know why I said no. A walk would have been very nice. Who was I punishing?

CHAPTER 4

Six years slid by with few surprises, which I suppose is, all things considered, a good thing, since surprises more often than not deliver the kind of news you can do without. My one impressive surprise was that Barry hadn't left me. Like a hypochondriac, I was anxious a good deal of the time: would the "blister" turn out to be malignant? As for my legal mate, she hung on as well; I was going to add "wouldn't you know?" But I admit that I was more comfortable in my eccentric situation than, in hindsight, I should have been, the comfort arising from my success in pulling off what some might call a double life—although, at the time, I didn't think of it as double. *Doubled* maybe, which is one, as in a double serving of mashed potatoes, while *double* is two—twins or vision or scoops of ice cream.

Phyllis was always an active presence, never reluctant to speak her mind—that is, when a cogent thought was in the forefront. She still withheld that last bit of herself, the part that informed her basic temperament, the thing about a person that cannot be changed, as in "shy" or "sweet" or "argumentative." She made it clear that she expected to have sex several times a week (sometimes I thought that for her sex was like a sort of beauty treatment or vitamin regime). And I had no trouble getting it up; my sex drive was apparently more catholic than parochial. Phyllis rarely talked during the act but made little humming noises indicating pleasure. She often complimented me on making her feel good. This was, to say the least, accidental. Not that I didn't want to please her, but when we were making love it would not be too difficult to imagine who I was thinking about. Let's say the difference between applesauce and raspberry mousse.

By 1954, a lot had happened in the world beyond my home, beyond my office. The so-called Cold War had hardened into slabs of seemingly impenetrable ice. Phyllis went berserk when the Rosenbergs were executed, absolutely convinced of their innocence. She inveighed against the people in charge just as she had when they put Alger Hiss behind bars for perjury a couple of years earlier. Phyllis wasn't just a leftist ideologue; she was profoundly suspicious of Republicans, whom she called "skunks," "liars," and when really riled up, "pigs." It wasn't all that easy having a conversation with her, partly because of the heat she generated and partly because, as I told her once or twice when I couldn't help myself, that she was a broken record. Of course I agreed with most of her views, but felt I had to take a moderating stance or our life at home would have sounded like Speakers' Corner in Hyde Park and the children would have fled. Wisely, Barry wouldn't talk about Phyllis with me except in the vaguest terms.

If there are ironies to be found in this story—and I don't turn to this concept lightly as I don't think it should be wasted on mere coincidence—they were that, as left-wing as Phyllis was, my money-making and close pal, Edgar Fleming (I considered myself the midwife of his literary offspring), was about as right-wing as one could get without falling off into the void. Whenever Fleming came to our house for dinner, I would make Phyllis swear that she wouldn't approach any subject that might lead to a food fight. More than once I had told Fleming about Phyllis' politics, making her sound a little maniacal. "Please," I said to him, "if you want to have a good time, stay away from anything that smells remotely like politics. You know Phyllis."

Fleming was more than willing; he didn't like to be harangued while eating his roast lamb and lyonnaise potatoes. Who would?

Edgar Fleming and I were still firm friends. For a man whose politics and attitudes contrasted sharply with my own, he still charmed me with his lack of pretension, his sense of the ridiculous, and his openness to other people. Also his amazing literary output. This was not inconsequential. We often met over lunch. If I was pressed for time we met at a restaurant near my office; if not, we went to the Orange Club. I shared Phyllis' view that this restrictive policy was stupid, especially considering that every last one of us had come this close to being wiped out entirely, and that the fine distinction between Russian and German Jews was invisible to everyone who wasn't Jewish. But I liked the Orange Club, as much for its muted atmosphere, purchased with a lot of money, as for its excellent menu and first-rate staff. You don't get that kind of quiet in a bus terminal. At the Orange Club, there was no check-grabbing between me and Fleming. The meal was automatically charged to me, and I then automatically put in for it on my generous expense account. This is the way it was done. Editor plies author with food and drink in a gesture of continued friendship and an ongoing business relationship. Fleming seemed to enjoy this unusual place near the peak of New York society's mountain but destined never to reach the pinnacle—at least not until both of us were long gone and Jews were accepted like other white men, and maybe not even then. But who knew, sometime in the future New York might even elect a Jewish mayor.

Fleming reached for a warm, chubby little roll, sprinkled with salt. He was still single and seemed in no hurry to alter his life. His attitude was, "Why buy a cow when milk is so cheap?" Fleming drank more than his share of milk. He had not quite symmetrical features and penetrating eyes that seemed to drive a wedge between girls and their scruples.

Fleming was what some called a "cocksman," a term I didn't especially like but which he didn't seem to mind. During the war, when we worked in the same outfit, some of Fleming's girls hung around outside the front doors while others sent him presents—tie clips, handkerchiefs, Gene Krupa records, net bags full of pecans. I never saw him wear a tie clip.

I had been around novelists long enough to know that most of them were not endowed with an abundance of scruples themselves. Among their number were adulterers, bashers, perpetrators of black eyes and swollen lips, neglecters of children and fathers of bastards, often unacknowledged. The male novelist was a wild man or a pathological loner. The female exhibited nymphomania, rampant narcissism, kinky behavior. I should not be taken too seriously. A lot of novelists were pussycats, easy to deal with, pathetically easy to please, eager for editorial criticism and long expensive lunches.

I'm certain Fleming enjoyed his reputation as a ladies' man even though it implied that he wasn't a genuinely serious person. But he was so confident of his powers that it didn't matter a bit what his reputation was like when it didn't concern his work. After all, he said, "Hemingway hunts mountain lions, I hunt girls."

Fleming applied butter to his roll and said, "I'm getting married, Walt."

"You're *what?*"

"Yes, my friend, I'm finally going to take the plunge. Don't you agree it's about time. I'm not getting any younger. Excuse the cliché."

I asked him who the girl was.

"I don't think you know her. Her name's Mary. Mary Severance. That's her married name. Her maiden name was Clark, I think. Yes, I'm sure. Mary Clark. Spence and Wellesley."

"She's divorced?" I was trying to absorb this bit of news; I had Fleming figured for someone who would never marry.

"A few months ago," he said. "Husband threw her against the wall. She doesn't weigh very much. He's a nasty fellow, nasty habits. Probably married her for her money. People do that, you know."

In the pause that followed I made a mental note to have Fleming's next novel vetted by a lawyer. Who knew what he might toss into it to get back at his ladylove's ex.

A waiter appeared stealthily at the table. Pointing to the menu, Fleming ordered jellied madrilène—"please make sure it's not too set"—the veal marsala, roast potatoes, and "that excellent endive salad of yours. No dessert. A cup of Italian coffee—you have Italian coffee?"

"Espresso, sir."

After taking our orders the waiter moved gravely toward the kitchen, entering it through leather-skinned swinging doors.

How could you not like it?

Fleming spent the next several minutes complaining about what he viewed as a doleful trend in fiction. "All these guys seem to want to do is expose their precious little psyches. 'Look at how I'm suffering,'" he said. "People don't want to read that shit, they want to read about life and death, criminal activity. Want to stir them up? Give them a good strong dose of violence."

I made the mistake of mentioning Jane Austen and Virginia Woolf. The look on Fleming's face said, *For crissake, we're not talking about a quilting bee or a sewing circle. We're talking about muscle.*

"Yes," I said, "you're probably right. What about that Ellison book?"

"*Invisible Man*? An exception. That's one smart Negro."

"Who would have thought?" I said. I don't know whether he picked up on my sarcasm. I was annoyed at him but I shouldn't have been surprised; this kind of thing came out of his mouth all too often. Phyllis, as I said, had a hard time keeping her expressive mouth shut. Barry, who had never officially met Fleming or shaken his hand, though he had hung his coat up in the hall closet and put his hat on the hat shelf, wrote him off as a troglodyte. "What would he do if he found out about you and me?" he said.

"I don't know," I said. "Probably never speak to me again. Funny, isn't it, how much bigger and better his fictional characters are than he is. Where do they come from?"

"He makes it up?" Barry said.

While I was retrieving these small items of recent history, Fleming was filling me in on the current changes in his life. "I don't really want Mary's former marriage to end up in Leonard Lyons' column so just keep that under your hat. The days of open scandal may be long past, but Mary and her family are mucho touchy about this divorce business. Her father's livid. Hardly talks to her, blames her for marrying a brute. Only thing we agree about is we both voted for Eisenhower. That's not such a big deal; everybody else did too."

I asked him how long he had known Mary, how they had met, etcetera, etcetera, the usual basics that only skim the surface but people are eager to learn anyway. He had known her for more than a year—which surprised me, as he hadn't mentioned her until today. No one knew about their romance except her sister, since they had met at a party at her sister's apartment, overlooking Central Park, prime real estate. The sister was married to Fleming's lawyer—all very incestuous, if you ask me. "From the nineteenth floor you can't see the bums and perverts engaging in their disagreeable activities. It's all a beautiful green blur."

As Fleming continued to unveil his fiancée, it was clear that Mary was what some would have called "top drawer," possessing not necessarily money but social status. She knew her way around New York along with the Astors and the Schuylers, the kind of woman who frequented Elizabeth Arden's Red Door salon on Fifth Avenue at least once a week to be "done," exiting with hair so sleek and smooth it looked like yellow marble. She sat on the boards of several cultural institutions like the Whitney and the New York City Opera. I figured she must also be loaded, because as neither an artist nor a musician she had to have something bankable to recommend her. There was no stopping Fleming now. From what he said I gathered that Mary's father, an oil company executive, had promised to leave her and her sister a considerable collection of paintings and drawings, among them a Cézanne and a Braque. He ended with "and she has splendid teeth." One would hope, I thought loftily, for nothing less. The longer he talked the more I felt I might have to adjust to a new and different man from the one I had met a decade earlier. Had he changed or had the real Edgar Fleming fought his way to the surface after almost fifty years?

"When do I get to meet this incredible lady?" I said.

"Her sister, the one I told you about, is giving us a little party in a couple of weeks. You're the first person I'm asking—aside from family. I want to make sure you're there. You're family. I feel that way anyway." He looked down at his veal, obviously unused to anything that came close to sentimentality. And I have to admit I was startled. I knew he was attached to me as most authors are to their editors, look to them for all kinds of things that have nothing to do with words on a page. But this family thing came out of the blue.

I thanked him, somewhat clumsily, and thanked him again and said of course I'd be there. Wild horses, etcetera.

On the day of the party, a Friday, I came home from work early, took a shower, and discovering that Phyllis was not there yet and the children not home from school, I went upstairs to visit Barry.

Barry sat at his desk, writing in a large notebook, the kind you use to take notes in class.

I asked him what he was writing.

"My journal. You know I keep a journal."

"I guess," I said. I wasn't all that fond of this habit; it made me uneasy. Did Barry fancy himself a writer and would he ask me to read it with a critical eye? Or supposing someone found it and read it? Or—the worst possible case—supposing he used it to blackmail me? Would they believe him? Maybe not, maybe they'd figure he was writing a novel and all these juicy bits were products of a lively imagination. In any case, I didn't like the idea of a written record of Barry's life because his life was my life. I was the opposite of "torn," which is the way you render feeling two ways at once, pulled by both equally so that you're paralyzed. I wasn't torn, I was compacted. The lives I led, the one sanctimoniously sanctioned, the other harshly outlawed, had melded together. Often, when I woke up in the morning, I thought the person next to me, still asleep, was Barry, not Phyllis. I told myself to for crissake keep Oscar Wilde in mind; his punishment for loving men rather than women was worse than that meted out to embezzlers. The punishment for engaging in man to man sex was worse in this country than in the Soviet Union. As I stood there watching Barry cap his fountain pen, close the notebook and slide it into the drawer, I was struck a glancing blow by the lunatic aspect of my adventure. But it didn't leave a mark; I wasn't interested, then, in calculating risk. To be candid, my libido was more potent than my prudence. I was no longer good old Walter Samson who never skipped a class in school, who always did his homework, who never went out back (actually, we had no "back") to smoke cigarettes with the guys, who never used a prostitute or called in sick when he wasn't, and who only once in his life stole something—a pink Spaldine from Woolworth's. And then he gave it back!

"I have thoughts and feelings I need to express," Barry said to me. "Sometimes I forget them so I write them down while they're still red hot. Hot off the griddle." With this, he placed his palm on the notebook. "Ouch!"

"You better be careful with that thing," I said. Sometimes his lighthearted attitude toward danger annoyed me. But then his risk was nothing compared to mine. He was a kept man; I was the keeper and the keeper's the one who gets into the most trouble.

"Lock and key," Barry said, pointing to a tiny lock in the drawer with a tiny key, which he turned, withdrew, and put in a pocket.

He seemed to have put an end to this topic. "I smell like lavender," I said. "Phyllis buys this English soap you couldn't get during the war. Yardley."

Barry got up and embraced me while I buried my chin in the cup-like scoop above his collarbone. I pulled in as much air as I could, inhaling his smell, perspiration, his Kreml, and aftershave, a heady mix which had lavender all beat to hell. "You're the best," I said, knowing he preferred to stay away from mawkishness, and tried to keep my ardor from overflowing. "Promise me you won't leave . . ."

"Promise," he said, I thought a little too quickly. Barry was the more loved of the two of us and that gave him a dangerous advantage. I tried to imagine life without him. I couldn't do it. I saw only blackness.

I told Barry I could only stay a few minutes. There was this party for my author, Ed Fleming. It would no doubt be swarming with fat cats and a discrete sprinkling of men and women whose names appeared in Cholly Knickerbocker's and Leonard Lyons' gossip columns. A celebrated author was always a draw. Come meet Norman Mailer's fiancée, see John Steinbeck stand on his hands, come hear James Michener talk about the Cold War. There would also be a scattering of olde New York Society, gaunt ladies and swollen men. I enjoyed these sorts of events—up to a point and that point was generally reached when I realized that I was nodding and smiling while someone I didn't know was talking at me about a subject I had no interest in—like sailing or golf—or didn't want to talk about—like Communism or the weather. A certain notoriety would cling to me simply by having been present at one of the "important" social gatherings of the year, and I would thereafter be taken note of as a member of the crème de la crème—as if anyone really cared.

I began to complain to Barry that as soon as it was known that I was Fleming's editor I would attract any number of would-be moths, dying to tell me about the book other people told them they should write. Barry stopped me. "That's your job, man," he said. "Stop feeling sorry for yourself."

I told him that Phyllis had bought a new outfit for the party. Bergdorf's, where I believe half the price of the dress is atmosphere. She would wear high-heeled open sandals and a purse so slim it could hold only a Kleenex and a folded-up five-dollar bill for emergencies. "And you know how she gets when she's had a couple. Her tongue takes over and she goes full throttle. Anyone in her way, watch out!"

"Your wife's got style," Barry said. "It's her own style. Sort of like that chanteuse, Hildegard. Everybody loves Hildegard."

I had to admit that Phyllis' style was most certainly her own; she copied no one.

"Is that so bad?" Barry said, nuzzling my neck. "Look, Walt, you don't have to prove you love me by bad-mouthing your wife. How would you like to *be* her?"

"Unthinkable," I said. "I cannot make that leap."

As usual, when I found myself in a group of people most of whom I didn't know, I tensed up, as if waiting for a doctor's needle to do its thing. My prediction about the makeup of the guest list was more or less accurate. So I drank too much. I finished off a whiskey sour, then went ahead and ordered another, patiently waiting my turn at an amazing bar where they had just about every spirit anyone could possibly ask for. A man I didn't recognize said hello to me and I said hello back, trying to figure out if we knew each other or whether he was just being friendly, which most of the guests weren't. The second drink produced a tingly feeling and made me forget to care that I didn't feel happy. Phyllis was nowhere to be seen. She was never shy like me. My brow began to bring forth tiny droplets of perspiration. The room we were in—I assumed it was the living room—was easily thirty feet long, with windows over Fifth Avenue, and elaborately draped with rose-colored brocade embedded with gold threads. On the walls were paintings and drawings Fleming had told me about. I wanted to go up to them and stand just inches away from their surfaces and look closely, but I didn't want to seem like a hick who had never seen a Modigliani or a Dufy or a Sisley before.

I wandered through an arched opening into a somewhat smaller room where I saw Phyllis holding forth. People were listening to her, actually standing at a safe distance, but listening. I couldn't quite make out what she was talking about, but I realized that she had misjudged her audience, most of which was looking at its shoes. She was probably talking about Senator McCarthy or Roy Cohn, who she would happily have dismembered if she thought she could get away with it. I wondered what sort of impulse pushes a person who wants everyone to listen to them. At home, Phyllis had a built-in audience. And maybe she didn't notice the eye-rolling that went on between her children when she mounted one of her hobbyhorses. They were not the sort of children who would want to make their mother feel bad;

they had been taught to be polite. I could catch only a few words but they were loaded words: "destructive," "nasty," "mean-spirited," "fungus." Fungus? It was obvious she too had been drinking more than she ought to. She claimed she was allergic to alcohol but I didn't buy that; she simply couldn't take more than one drink without a large chunk of her judgment falling off. I felt sorry for her, not so much because she couldn't help doing what she was doing, but because she didn't seem to realize how poorly her lecture was going over.

I walked out of earshot. I wanted another drink but told myself that I should wait until I got home. Let no one accuse me of not having self-discipline. At this point in my self-congratulations, Mary's sister came up to me. She stood so close to me I could feel her breath on my cheek. "In case you didn't know," she said, "I'm your hostess." Was she scolding me because I hadn't greeted her earlier with a handshake? She was wearing a black velvet band across the top of her head. Was it meant to keep her yellow hair on her head. The thought made me smile. She said she was glad I seemed to be having a good time. She had that rocks-in-the mouth accent like FDR and all the Spence and Chapin ladies I had ever known. "I understand you're Edgar's publisher," she said. She twinkled her blue eyes at me.

I explained that I was his editor, not his publisher, and she asked me to explain the difference, which I did. The one has to do solely with content, the other with content plus the money involved in producing the actual book. "I see," she said. "Now I know." She seemed delighted, as if grasping a difficult theory in quantum mechanics. "And I always thought they were the same thing. Editor, publisher, publisher editor."

As for her sister, the bride-to-be, she was slim, long of limb, also blond but no velvet band. She was wearing a double strand of pearls and a black dress made of something soft and silky. Around her waist was a wide, patent leather belt pulled in so tightly it must have pinched her flesh. She wore the kind of smile that looked as if it could never be altered in any way, no matter what happened. It was just *there*, like the cat's in *Alice*. It would be there when she washed her face, wrote a check, walked into the dentist's office, engaged in sex. She exuded well-being, promise. And why not? She had hooked a rare fish in Fleming. He was a successful writer, which made it possible to overlook the fact that he was the son of a railroad conductor; it took him clear out of the worker category and put him in with the other artists: Olivier, Calder, José Limón, et al. He carried his fame lightly and handsomely, like a movie star who's counting on everyone's looking at him.

Mary said she was "thrilled" to meet me at last. "I've been so wanting to meet the man who discovered, well not exactly discovered, but helped bring to light, Edgar's amazing talent. I'm so proud of him. Don't you think he's the best writer in the world? He shows me his writings before he's even finished. Did you know that? And he asks my opinion! That's a total laugh, isn't it? I mean what do I know about that sort of thing? But I do know that when my little old mind begins to wander it's not a good sign. And I tell him, too. But it never ever wanders when I'm reading something Edgar wrote. The other night I stayed up till three in the morning reading the one he's writing now. The one about the Russian woman who kills the FBI agent in that mercantile place. Honestly, it sounds as if he'd worked there all his life. It's completely realistic. Do you think he's going to write the great American novel? I do!"

I couldn't think of anything to say so I just smiled.

"I'm so glad you agree with me," she said. I had the funny feeling that while she'd been carrying on, her little old mind was wandering. Even so, she kept her blue eyes on my face, a lock.

Fleming came over to join us. "I see you two have been getting to know each other." Quick flick of eyes from Mary to me and back. "Isn't she a charmer? I told you. Looks like Grace Kelly, only more so. You know what I mean."

"Grace Kelly?" Mary said. "I don't see it."

Fleming grabbed Mary around the waist and gave a mighty tug. She looked startled, lost some of her balance, and put her hand to her hair, as if to make sure it was still there. "Eddie, sweetie, you're such a bear!" She didn't look exactly pleased.

I began to have a good time, just chatting without thought or topic, the booze easing my uneasiness. I talked briefly to a youngish man who, when he found out what I did for a living, told me he was writing a book about his experience as an ambulance driver during the war and, amazing myself, I asked him to send it to me.

Phyllis said she wanted to leave. "These people are troglodytes. One of them said they weren't allowed to mention FDR's name in their house. They had to pay a fine. What kind of friends do you have?"

I reminded her that Edgar Fleming was my best and most lucrative author. "Besides, we've been friends since '44. So he's marrying the enemy. You don't have to live with him."

"Doesn't it matter to you?" she said, as we rode down in the elevator, paying no attention to its operator, whose back was to us and who no doubt relished some of the talk he heard on the trips up and down, up and down.

"Not really," I said. "What matters is his prose and his energy. That's all I really care about." This wasn't altogether true, but I'd found that if I made stark black or white statements I was more likely to get off easier than if I had argued each little point with her, peeling it, testing it, twisting it.

On the way home, with Barry at the wheel, Phyllis was saying something in her urgent voice. It was hard to focus on what she was saying because I was mesmerized by the back of Barry's head, where his beautiful black hairs came together over the exact middle of his neck, an arrow pointing down towards the site of love.

"I don't think you're listening to me," Phyllis said. "I just said I want to go back to work."

"Why now?" I said, forcing myself to concentrate.

"It was all those so-called women of leisure, they gave me the creeps. All they do is sit on boards and have their hair and nails done. That's not me, Walt, you know that. I'm bored at home. I can read just so many books. I'm wasting my time."

"You're not wasting your time," I said. "You're a mother. Remember Henry and Kate?"

"For heaven's sake, Walter, you sound like some old fool. What did I go to Bryn Mawr for? Why did I take art history and French literature? So I could plan my children's meals? So I can find my way around carpet showrooms? You try it, just for a week. You'd go nuts."

I sighed, trying hard to put myself in her place. It wasn't easy. Isn't that what women did? "What did you have in mind?"

"The same thing. You know, WNYC. Preparing scripts for the guys who read the news, book guests, all-around help for everybody. Not much money there but I loved the work."

I pointed out that she hadn't worked at the station for almost fifteen years. Lots of changes in that time. Television, the Cold War, Marlon Brando, that new kind of acting where you pretended you weren't acting, blacklists. Books with blunt sex in them. Dirty words. I was aware that I was throwing cold water on her plan without the slightest justification for doing so. Why shouldn't the old girl go back to work? Did I have a trace of atavistic caveman? Man hunts woman cooks. It was nonsense. Besides, if she had a job and was out of the house, my own life would be easier. I stared at the motionless head in front of me and turned my hands into fists to keep me from reaching out and stroking him from behind. *Oh my god I can't stand it.*

I told my wife that she should do what felt right for her, she should go ahead and work again. "In any case, I can't stop you. This is 1954."

"And why on earth would you want to stop me? "Phyllis said. "Honestly, Walt, sometimes I haven't the faintest idea what goes on inside your head."

A wave of self-pity washed over me and nearly cut off my supply of air. Only the thought of Barry waiting for a good-night hug and kiss kept me from throwing out my arm and smashing Phyllis in the face. I had never before felt this kind of fury and it frightened me; I didn't know what to do with it. I must have shown some of this on my face because Phyllis said, "Poor dear. You're tired. I promise you I won't turn into one of those man-eating bitches. Once they get a bite of the big world they feel they don't have to be decent wives and mothers anymore. I'll be home for dinner every night, I promise. I'll help the children with their homework."

My self-pity had given way to guilt and I reached for Phyllis' hand. It was cold and silky. I gave it a squeeze and withdrew before she had a chance to squeeze back.

When we reached the house Barry sprang from the driver's seat and hurried around to the rear door, which he held open for us. Phyllis thanked him with the polite tone she used when talking to anyone who worked for her.

"Yes, ma'am, Will that be all?"

"That's all for tonight, Barry. I'll need you tomorrow morning at ten-fifteen."

Barry said yes ma'am again. Following Phyllis from the curb to the front door, I looked at Barry with love and wonderment while his eyes flickered with amusement. I adored this man whose mind never traveled very far but whose body gave me extreme pleasure, the sort of pleasure I wasn't sure I deserved.

While Phyllis was getting ready for bed, I told her that I had to draft a letter that needed to go out first thing in the morning.

"Why do you always work so late?" she said. She stood near the bed, wearing a nightgown that reached her ankles and emphasized her considerable belly.

"I get some of my best ideas at night," I said. "I won't be long."

"Right." She pulled back the covers and lay down. "By the way, did I tell you I'm glad now you insisted on hiring Barry. He's very reliable. I wonder, does he have a girl-friend? I certainly hope so, good-looking man like that. Does he remind you of Montgomery Clift?"

Bingo! "Not in the slightest," I said. "And I don't know whether he has a girlfriend. He doesn't confide in me."

Phyllis looked at me blankly.

"I somehow doubt it," I said, regretting it the moment the words left my mouth.

"Why do you say that?" she said.

"I don't know. He seems to enjoy his own company. I'm probably wrong, he probably has a thousand ladies hankering for him. Anyway, it's none of our business. And about my late hours. You should be used to it by now."

"Well, I'm not."

⟜

"Did you by any chance hear what she had to say about going back to work?"

I had tiptoed upstairs and was standing inside Barry's room, where we were nuzzling each other. Barry thought it was a fine idea. Too many women were just lazy, why shouldn't they work in an office or whatever if they had someone else to do their domestic dirty work? We were whispering because cook and maid were in their rooms.

Somehow, after all this time, we had still evaded detection. Grete and Marie knew nothing about Barry and me. At least we were fairly sure about this. On the other hand, maybe there were suspicious nighttime noises, creaks on the stairs, doors closing and opening—and just hadn't let on. Or maybe they were gathering evidence to do me evil in some quiet, diabolical manner. My mind went swiftly down the paranoid trail until I stopped it abruptly. The master was humping his chauffeur—happily. If this meant taking risks, that's the way it was going to be.

"Your old lady's got balls," Barry said. "She's okay. I like that in a woman."

"And you've got some cheek," I said. "Is that any way to talk to your employer?"

"You love it, you old cocksucker."

CHAPTER 5

Edgar Fleming asked me to be best man at his wedding. This happened near the end of one of our lunch meetings, which were part social, part business, the two functions having, in our case, become so melded that you couldn't have pulled them apart. Generally, I let Fleming do most of the talking; Edgar Fleming didn't at all mind talking about himself. There was always a bit of news, his run-in with Spyros Skouras, his flirtation with Tallulah Bankhead, his night out with William Faulkner or Red Warren drinking whiskey in some West Village dive. He had somehow transformed himself into an entertainer and intellectual guru, a kind of Dick Cavett or Bill Buckley without the microphone or camera. When he asked me to stand up with him at his wedding, my hand with the coffee cup in it stopped halfway to my mouth.

"Well," I said, putting down the cup. "I'm flattered, naturally, but what about your brother? Don't you want to ask him?"

"Grant and I are on the outs this year. Even years we're on the outs, odd years we're civil to each other—barely. Too much wailing about McCarthy. I can't take it; I mean he's a broken record. He and I don't exactly see eye to eye about what's going on in the State Department and elsewhere in D.C. Grant's a screenwriter. Last one he did was for Fred MacMurray and Barbara Stanwyck. It wasn't too shoddy. He'd be okay if it wasn't for his goddamn hobbyhorse. Grant's been blacklisted so he peddles his wares under a pseudonym, something like Lucky Jonas. Who's going to believe that? Funny, we're in the same racket but worlds apart in our thinking. Actually, by not asking him, I spare him the embarrassment of saying no."

I asked Fleming whether Grant was going to be asked to the wedding.

"I haven't made up my mind on that one."

A little earlier Fleming and I had been talking about his new novel. He pushed them out like a champion laying-hen. You would think, given these circumstances, that they would lose their freshness and energy after a while, but he managed to keep his readers rapt, begging for more. He had begun to use some characters in more than one book. One of these was Aubrey Galliston, a kind of armchair detective-philosopher whom his readers responded to as if he was a real flesh-and-blood person: "Oh, I absolutely love Aubrey, don't you just love him?" But our discussion was really perfunctory, because Fleming needed almost no coaching; he would create an outline, keep the action of a novel within one short time period, say a week or two, and then account for the action on every single day covered. Work-wise, Fleming was a Prussian.

Years before, I had discovered that it was futile to try to match an author with his work. If you loved his book, you might be very disappointed to discover a roaring narcissist, a drunk, a compulsive womanizer, or any of a number of disagreeable types. Or you might meet a really nice guy, someone you want to make a friend of. There was no predicting which it would be. If this seems hard to credit, just think of an actor who plays the part of an axe murderer. You don't confuse the actor and his role. It's a good idea not to confuse the author with his fiction.

So Fleming was nothing like most of his characters. Ask him where they came from and he would likely say, "I make them up."

As we rose to leave, Fleming clapped me on the shoulder and told me how glad he was that I was going to be his best man. I had some misgivings, centered mainly on the blacklisted brother whose nose might be out of joint.

⌦

ABOUT MARRIAGE, an odd business in which patience is an absolute necessity and an attitude of inertia a definite plus. What, after all, is truly worth screaming and yelling about? My *amour propre*? Your precious longings? Forget it. If you marry you have to decide to put up with a difficult situation in which at least half of a man's freedom is compromised. Every so often I stopped to consider why I married Phyllis. In spite of my experience as a youth at camp, I considered myself heterosexual—so let's get that out of the way at the start. I was attracted to her, not so much to her sexual promise as to her spirit, which caught most people's attention. But, think of it, love is nature's cruel joke: you see your mate-to-be in a light so flattering, so pearly, it can't be—and isn't—real. By the time the luster has worn off, it's too late.

Phyllis was an original. As it happened, she remained that way, but this trait isn't quite so appealing after you've lived with it for twenty years. You would like a little less singularity, a little more harmony.

Phyllis graduated from Hunter College in 1927 and went straight to work. This put her in a category of less than one percent of her American sisters. She edited an in-house newspaper for the Hearst Corporation. It was several steps up from an entry-level job, and according to her she worked very hard at it, producing a mimeographed, stapled-together, newsy, weekly document that went to—and was presumably read by—every employee in the company. After that she went to work for the Radio Corporation of America in their advertising department, and then to radio station WNYC, the "voice" of New York City and the place she was working when we met. So Phyllis and I were basically in the same line of work in spite of the fact that for ladies to get this sort of job was extremely difficult and rare as diamonds in the mud. I knew an assistant editor at Griffin House, for example, who manned the telephone switchboard during lunch hours even though she had earned a Phi Beta Kappa at Radcliffe. She said, "I don't mind, really, I think it's sort of fun. You get to listen in on conversations." Idiot!

Phyllis had a way of persuading the hesitant that she was the absolutely right person—especially if she was dealing with a man. I don't mean she flirted or slept her way into rooms other ladies couldn't enter. There probably was an element of coquetry in her approach, but that wasn't the main ingredient of her success. It was her self-confidence and a mastery of several critical facts that demonstrated she knew what she was talking about.

Phyllis had an abundance of energy and enthusiasms and didn't mind taking risks. Mentally, I set her against my mother who generally steered away from anything odd or risky. In our marriage Phyllis was usually the one who initiated things—from choosing where we lived, to how we spent our money, to sex. Like our switchboard girl, I didn't really mind; it left me more time to make decisions at work, something I enjoyed very much. Which manuscript to get behind, whether to let the production people do the jacket picture or send it to an outside professional, how to write the jacket copy, etc. I was good at taking a situation apart and putting it back together again in a different configuration. I was able to judge with fair accuracy the ultimate consequences of my choices. At home I was limp.

So it's easy to understand why my feelings about weddings were, to say the least, ambiguous. The part of me that was romantic—the part I lavished on Barry—enjoyed seeing four starry eyes locked in early marital bliss. The part of me that had soured made me want to rise up at the ceremony itself—like Mr. Rochester's brother-in-law in *Jane Eyre*—and yell "Stop!"

Phyllis said, "What do you think I should wear to the wedding?"

I knew she didn't expect me to answer; she was already going over her filmy wardrobe, all neatly lined up in her scented closet (lavender), each waiting to be next to her warm skin.

"Not black," I said. "Or white. White's for the bride."

"I know that, Walt, who wears black to a wedding?"

I thought this was an interesting conceit and I could see that many might be tempted. Then Phyllis was saying that we had to get them something "really nice." I reminded her that I could put the price of the item on my expense account, but in the end I didn't. I wanted to pay for it myself.

"By really nice do you mean expensive?"

"Natch," she said. "I thought maybe something from Jensen's, silver, silver candlesticks, or maybe a glass tray. They mold them into different shapes. Why don't I get one for us?"

I told her to go ahead and find something "really nice," hoping she would pick up on my sarcasm.

She ended up getting a silver platter with the bride and groom's initials intertwined in the center so that they resembled a bird. So pretty, so useless. It cost three hundred bucks but I didn't begrudge the money she spent on it; Fleming was my golden goose. It was Fleming who was responsible for my own bright arc at Griffin House.

❧

THE WEDDING was to take place in St. James' Episcopal Church on Madison Avenue, where many of New York's smartest showed up every Sunday, sang standard Anglican hymns, and listened to a sermon that more often made them feel better rather than more anxious or guilty—no hellfire or brimstone. The minister would be one of those silver-haired prep-school types with wonderful diction and a deep, reassuring voice. The church itself was a darkish, soaring structure, traditional in ambiance, entirely suited to the congregation—and vice versa. One of my cousins, bless her, switched religions from Hebrew to Episcopalian and became a member of St. James'. I admired her guts but didn't appreciate what turned out to be a convincing disguise. Her second husband was a minister.

On the day of the wedding, a Saturday, I left the house after eating a light lunch. Phyllis was trying on dresses, one after the other. "I wish I'd bought that little green number at Bendel's," she said.

"Why didn't you?"

"It did nothing for my eyes," she said, twitching her body in front of the full-length mirror. "Does it make my bottom look fat?"

"Of course not," I said. "You do not have a fat bottom."

"Why does he want you there so early?"

"Nervous groom," I said.

The engraved wedding invitation, with self-addressed envelope and a small square of tissue paper, said that the ceremony would begin at four-thirty. It was a warm day in mid-April. Phyllis wore a cobalt blue dress with one of her five-foot-long scarves and a waist-length mink cape, which was fashionable but not Phyllis' style. I'd never seen it before. "You like it?" she asked.

"I'm not sure. When did you buy it?"

"I didn't. My sister lent it to me."

I reminded her what time the wedding was called for. "They'll start on time. It's like a high school class. The bell rings, we all sit down. Teacher's already there."

"What are you talking about?"

I didn't answer.

"Well, I'll see you later, at the church I suppose. I'll take the car," she said. "You don't mind, do you?"

Mind? Yes, I minded. But I didn't say so. I would walk and she would get to be within a closed space with the love of my life.

Fleming had kept his first and only apartment, which was on Third Avenue and Fifty-Third Street. It was a third-floor walk-up with a minuscule kitchen he rarely used, preferring to eat out. He had a small workroom for his desk, typewriter, and books, a serious room without ruffles of any sort. He didn't own a television set but he did have an old record player on which he played mostly swing, just as I did. Tommy Dorsey, Frank Sinatra, Earl "Fatha" Hynes. When he gave a party he would pack the place and serve Johnny Walker Black and Bombay gin and a couple of bowls of potato chips. Sometimes there were fights after people got drunk, and once the police turned up and told him to pipe down, the neighbors were complaining. He could have lived almost anywhere, but he loved this apartment and his friends loved it too; it was what a Negro friend of his called "cool."

I climbed the three flights and rang the bell. Fleming answered. He was wearing a cotton robe over his boxers and a white tee shirt. His feet were bare. "Greetings, old chum," he said. "What can I get you to drink?" Clearly, there had been a party the night before; glasses were everywhere, some of them with drink still in them, others with cigarette butts floating like dead fish. The smell was powerful: smoke and whiskey and body heat, all of it stagnant. There was a pair of loafers near the window overlooking the Third Avenue El, which was slated to be demolished the following year.

I said, "I thought you weren't going to have a bachelor party."

"I wasn't, I didn't," he said. "This was an afterthought. Honestly."

A girl emerged from the tiny kitchen. She blinked, as if to get the sleep out of her eyes.

"You remember Betty Gilpin? From the steno pool?"

"Well, if he doesn't remember me I sure remember him," the girl said. She looked to be about forty, slightly shopworn and wearing a silk kimono, a kind of clichéd garment that made me think of Sadie Thompson, the sad heroine of *Rain*. "I'm not sure," I said.

"Betty wanted to come up here and join me for old time's sake. My last night of freedom, so to speak."

I remarked that it must have been quite a party, wondering why he hadn't asked me to join him.

"We got started after eleven," he said. "Some of the old gang just showed up."

It was an awkward moment for me but Fleming didn't seem the least disconcerted. Betty, meanwhile, went off somewhere, presumably to get dressed. Again, Fleming asked me if I'd like a drink, which I declined. He said he ought to get cracking but made no move to do so. Instead he went into the kitchen. "Shit! No clean glasses."

He invited me to take a seat while he showered. "You're a good egg to do this," he said over his shoulder. I wasn't sure what "this" referred to—being there now or being best man—or both. I felt uncomfortable in my new dinner jacket, probably because this was its first time out and it pinched me under the arms. I sat down and thought about Barry, wondering what he was doing. Was he lying on his back having a smoke and listening to the radio?

The daydream continued and then Betty came back, wearing a silk dress with flowers all over it.

"Can I mooch a cigarette from you? I'm all out."

To keep her company I lighted one for each of us. She told me she remembered me very well from during the war. "You were smart and quiet. Some of the guys looked up to you. I'll bet you didn't know that."

I shook my head. I not only hadn't known that. (I was certain they thought I was a prep school snob, which didn't make me the most popular man on board.) I also didn't believe her.

"Some of the girls thought you were pretty cute. You know, girls like the strong silent type. Gary Cooper, sort of like that."

"Come on, Betty, you know better than that."

"Better than what?" She began to gather up last night's debris, twitching her behind as she walked back and forth from the living room to the kitchen, smoking all the while.

I knew that all I had to do was stick my hand out as she passed by me, and I could have had her right there while Fleming was in the shower. But I found her about as appealing as a plate of boiled cauliflower. The waste of it! The flirtation, if you want to call it that, was all on her side, and I sensed that had I grabbed at this advantage she would have cared as much or as little as if I hadn't. It was all the same to her.

Fleming reemerged. He had on striped trousers and was struggling with the studs on a dress shirt. His black suspenders lay against his thighs. "Fucking shirt," he said. "Hey Betty, do you know how to do up these things?"

Betty helped him with the shirt. He lay his left hand across her backside and wiggled his fingers. The smile she gave him tried, I think, to convey a sense of irony, which I'm pretty sure Fleming did not share.

Eventually Fleming's three ushers, not including his brother, Grant, showed up. They looked like models for some smart brand of whiskey or cigarettes, and they had that air of privilege I associated with members of the New York Athletic Club. None of them looked remotely like a writer. The five of us stood around trying our best to be hearty, drinking and telling dirty, anti-marriage jokes until it was time to leave.

We persuaded a taxi driver to take all five of us, although he told us it was illegal. Fleming assured him he'd pay the fine if we were caught. We weren't caught. It was early enough so that no one had arrived at the church except those who had a part in the ceremony, and the flower arrangers, who were putting the finishing touches on long streams of wide satin ribbon punctuated by bunches of white and pink flowers. The three ushers took off to do their appointed tasks, and Fleming and I slipped into the godly green room where we were met by the minister inside clerical robes. He had a youthful, ruddy face and wire-rimmed glasses. I opened the door to the sanctuary a crack and looked out over the crowd. The place was packed. Baroque organ music started up quietly. The minister said, "Gentlemen, it's time," and asked me if I was sure I had the ring. Fleming had bought it at Cartier; the stone was an emerald-cut diamond half the size of a sugar cube, set in a platinum band. I had stuck it in the pocket of my jacket, where it formed a bulge. Fleming smiled encouragingly at me. I figured he was a little drunk.

We stepped into the sanctuary and waited, side by side (I actually could feel Fleming's heart pounding). Walking down the aisle ten feet in front of Mary and her father were two adorable blond children, the boy wearing short black velvet pants and the girl a stiff white dress that stood straight out like a dancer's tutu. Each of them carried a basket filled with flower petals which they had been instructed to distribute on the aisle floor like grain to a flock of chickens. Oohs and aahs floated around the church when these two angels appeared. The boy shot out his left leg and gave the girl a kick just below the hem of her costume. It was a hard kick; you could hear his leg connect with hers. The girl let out a shriek and dropped her basket. No one said a word. Fleming stiffened. There was the merest trace of a smile on his face. The girl began to bawl, the noise rising and echoing against the stone walls. A woman—presumably her mother—rushed over and picked up the child and dragged her off into a side aisle, where she continued to wail. With a slight rustle, the audience resettled itself and the ceremony went on as if nothing had happened. How I admired the restraint. Mary was released by her father, at which point Fleming moved from my side to hers, exactly as we had rehearsed it the day before. Five bridesmaids of varying sizes and shapes, every one stuffed into an identical pale pink dress with a wide satin belt, stood on the other side of the altar looking as self-conscious as if they were naked. One of them giggled, another seemed about to faint.

The minister took a long time blessing the couple, delivering a homily that recommended the joys and pleasures of family life, skipping over the honeymoon and all that that entails. He read from *The Book of Common Prayer*: "And here we offer and present unto thee, O Lord, ourselves, our souls and bodies, to be a reasonable, holy and *living* sacrifice unto thee." The word "reasonable" struck me as odd in its context, as odd as a lemon growing on an olive tree. He admonished Mary and Edgar not to seek happiness in worldly things—the usual grab bag of advice containing more than a grain of truth, but so well buried beneath threadbare rhetoric that I would guess some of the wedding guests missed it entirely. Fleming began to rock slightly on the balls of his feet, impatience seeping out of him like sweat. Mary was perfectly still. Finally, the minister got around to renaming them "Man and Wife." Fleming let out an audible sigh.

The organ struck up again and the couple turned and walked briskly back down the aisle, reversing direction. Mary smiled right and left and right again. Fleming looked as if he were glad to get this over. The guests rose with a creak here and a grunt there, and we all headed toward the back—or is it the front? I can never remember—and on to the reception.

This was held at the clubhouse of The Century Association, an all-male establishment founded in the nineteenth century and dedicated to helping the arts thrive in a society that seemed ever more prone to helping the businessman thrive. It was said that members were not allowed to talk to anyone in the press about the club, its membership or activities, on pain of expulsion. So the club had about it an air of mystery that made it seem something like the most sacrosanct of secret societies, like Yale's Skull and Bones. You enter, you're transformed. This was the first time I had been inside the club, and I half expected a robed ancient to blindfold me and walk me through fire and water while drums beat in the background. But as I said to Phyllis as we stood inside the glass doors, in the lobby—with its marble floors and double staircase—it was the twin of the Orange Club. "They're all alike," I said. "On the surface and deep down. Brothers in exclusion."

The reception was a cocktail party with a few canapés—pigs in blankets, chicken livers wrapped in greasy bacon, minuscule egg salad sandwiches. The bars—there were two of them, one at each end of a gallery halfway up to the second floor—were doing a brisk business. "You can tell it's not a Jewish wedding," I said. "Heavy on the booze, light on the food." Some of the guests, thirsty after a long after-noon, elbowed their way to where glasses and bottles were lined up in a neat phalanx. The bride, her train gathered up and hanging gracefully over her left arm, walked around chatting with small groups of her guests. Fleming did the same. Phyllis spotted a man she knew and went over to talk with him beneath a large pastel of a girl reading a book in a window seat with leafy trees on the other side of the window. This was not the place for abstract expressionism. Someone came up to me and asked if I played golf; I said, "I'm afraid not." He turned and left, presumably to find someone who did.

I looked at my watch and tried to decide how much longer I had to stay. Would there be speeches? Of course there would be speeches, and as best man, I would be expected to say something witty, edgy, and loving.

Just then I sensed a kind of stir in the crowd, and heard a yelp like that of a puppy whose tail has been caught in the screen door. In a flash, Fleming was at my side. "Get that man out of here," he said.

"What man?"

"Fred Forstman. Your boss."

"Ex-boss," I said.

"Okay then, ex-boss. Just get him out of here."

"What's he done?"

"He's smashed. He's getting just a bit too close to some of Mary's lady friends. He pinched my mother-in-law on the ass."

"Fred did that? You must be kidding."

"Mary's having a fit."

I wasn't all that surprised. But this was a matter not of category but of degree, and I figured the drugs he was taking to keep him upright had affected his judgment. I was amused but dared not show it; Fleming was very angry. He repeated his instructions. I'm not sure I was the one to remove Fred, but I went along with Fleming anyway. I remarked that anything can happen at a wedding and often does.

"Not at my wedding," Fleming said. "This guy's fucking out of control. Mary's not used to this sort of thing."

The two of us walked over to where Forstman was standing with a woman in a smart black dress, a small hat perched on her blond curls and a deep ravine between her breasts. Forstman practically had his face in the ravine. One of his hands was holding a golden drink, mostly gone. The other was restless at the end of its arm. I figured a couple of minutes more and the hand would have found a risky target. "Hey Fred," I said, "Wouldn't you like some fresh air?"

"No. Why? Helluva party. Hello my friend, my golden goose," he said to Fleming.

He turned back to the woman who, for reasons known only to herself, was still standing there. Maybe she liked it. Forstman might be old and sick but he had a young man's reckless nerve.

"Thanks, Fred, for the compliment. Now how about you and Walt and I take a little walk downstairs and outside. I think you've had enough party."

Forstman looked confused. "What's the matter? Did I commit an unseemly act? Have you met my new acquaintance here? What did you say your name was, honey? Hey, did you fellas know that Episcopal is a perfect anagram for Pepsi-Cola?"

The woman suddenly seemed to grasp what was happening. "I don't think that's particularly funny," she said. "I don't think you should joke about religion. And please excuse me." With that, she turned and walked away.

"It's not a joke," Forstman said. "It's an anagram. Oops!" Forstman got his feet wrapped around each other. "Where's Judy?" Judy was Mrs. Forstman.

We looked around and couldn't spot her. Fleming told me to take Forstman downstairs while he went to look for Judy.

"I must of done something," Forstman said softly, shaking his head. "Or else I've lost my touch. Where did you say you wanted me to go?"

We walked down the marble staircase. I retrieved Forstman's coat and hat from the cloakroom; he couldn't get his mind around what they looked like, so he had a hard time describing them. Just then Fleming brought Judy, who looked—I don't quite know which—mad or frightened, or maybe she couldn't choose between them. She asked her husband if he was alright. He assured her he was. "Just had one too many of those Century martinis," he said. "I think I'll go home now."

When we got back upstairs the crowd was still hanging in there, waiting for toasts to be made and cake to be cut.

Fleming remarked he hadn't known that Forstman had a drinking problem.

"I don't think he does," I said. "Do you know how sick he is? They've given him less than a year to live."

"All I know is he has no manners," Fleming said. "Let's not talk about it."

He was steaming. He seemed not to be able to shake it off. Fortunately, it was time for the toasts. I was called on first. I made the expected, unoriginal jokes about perennial bachelors greeted by polite laughter. I talked some about our experiences together in wartime Washington, made a passing reference to the Cold War (without moral inflection but with pointed reference to the bride and groom— "may there never develop," etc., etc.); and then partly to help Fleming get rid of the bad taste in his mouth, spoke briefly about how much this author meant to Griffin House and especially to Fred Forstman. "Fred, where are you?" I said. Heads swiveled, but of course he had left the premises. "Well," I said, winding up. "May Ed and Mary enjoy the life together that they deserve." Polite applause. Then Mary's father spoke and then his brother, Grant, who had shown up and was appropriately ambiguous while Fleming frowned.

Phyllis said, "I suppose you're ready to leave?"

"As a matter of fact I am. You?"

"I just met someone from the station. I'd like to stay and talk to him for a few minutes." She assumed I knew she meant WNYC.

I told her I didn't think I wanted to stay; the noise was getting to me and the feeling that I was trapped. She consented, and asked if I wouldn't mind taking a cab home so she could ride in the car with Barry. "Of course you can have the car," I said even as my heart was breaking.

❧

It was past eleven when Phyllis got home. No visit with my prince tonight. I was in bed reading one of Bruce Catton's books about the Civil War, rumored to be a top contender for this year's Pulitzer in non-fiction. It was a pretty good read and I kicked myself for not having made a larger offer when it was originally auctioned.

"Oh, you're still awake?" she said.

"Did you eat?"

"Those nasty little hors d'oeuvres?" she said. "No, I made myself a sandwich just now." There was a trace of something shiny on her chin. Why did I notice these things?

"Well," I said, "you certainly seemed to have enjoyed yourself. What a crowd! My father would have called half of it 'the enemy.'"

"You mean because most of them are Republicans? Sometimes—and you're probably not going to believe this— I can overlook that. Especially, you know, if it has something to do with me." She was peeling her clothes off as she talked. I pretended to look at her, but I threw a veil over my eyes so I wouldn't have to see the rolls and bumps and lumps; is there anything crueler than what time does to a female?

"I'm going to take a shower. My hair stinks of cigarette smoke."

Phyllis was a long showerer. I decided to take a chance that tonight's shower would be especially long. As soon as Phyllis was safely in the bathroom with the door closed, I sprinted upstairs for a goodnight hug and kiss. It turned out to be something more extended than a simple hug and kiss. When I came back downstairs, Phyllis was in bed with the bedside lamp turned off. Light from cars traveling our street striped the ceiling and were gone. In the dark, she asked me where I had been. Guilt made me irritated and rough. I told her that she knew I had some of my best ideas at night, why did she keep asking me the same question over and over again. I was writing a memo about the Civil

War if she really wanted to know; did she want to take a look at it.

"You don't have to jump down my throat," she said.

I muttered an apology as I slipped into bed beside her. I could feel her heat although none of our body parts were touching.

"That man at the reception I was talking to? He works at the station. He told me he was pretty sure I had the job."

"Congratulations," I said, wondering if she expected me to kiss her goodnight. She smelled like lavender, for me a very seductive odor. The guilt was draining away and a rush of benevolence came over me. Two people loved me. Most of us have only one, at best. I knew with perfect clarity that some might view my little arrangement as sick; but far from feeling sick I was energized by the variety of sexual experience open to me. It made me think hard about a lot of things I would not have had I lived as an ordinary husband and father. For example, after long consideration, I had decided that men and women used their brains differently. Even though Barry was queer, he thought like a man, he used his brain like a muscle. Most women didn't do this and I was pretty sure they couldn't have even if they wanted to.

CHAPTER 6

B arry's mother developed a fast-moving blood disease; and after living with considerable pain from it for nearly a year, died. I wanted to go to her funeral, but Barry persuaded me that my presence there would raise eyebrows, if not suspicion: did I want to take that risk? Barry was gloomy for weeks after his mother's death. I tried to cheer him up by telling him about the latest triumphs and flubs at Griffin House, but he wasn't interested in listening. My Sundays did not improve; all my words were under lock and key inside my head. The children, now awash in adolescence, had many friends, some of whom they brought home for a visit behind closed bedroom doors or, just as often, went out with, to the movies or ice skating at Gay Blades. Blue laws kept stores closed on Sunday so shopping was not an option. Kate and Henry were street-wise partly because Phyllis and I were more permissive than most parents. We agreed on this, as we did on several other basics. It was ironic (a much-abused word, but apt in this case) that here was a person with whom I shared key notions of how best to navigate through life, and yet I couldn't work up the requisite enthusiasm to love her the way I should. Sometimes, especially when I was tired or anxious, her round smooth-skinned face, her round smooth-skinned arms (thank god they were hairless; nothing repels me like a woman with hairy arms), her Renoiresque body, set my teeth on edge and I had to walk out of the room to keep from throttling her. It wasn't until I brought Barry into my life that I felt any real warmth toward my wife. A paradox? Not really, because when I fell in love with Barry I no longer had so much invested in my relationship with Phyllis, so I could more easily ignore the irritations that invade every marriage.

As for letting the children make a lot of their own decisions, it paid off because they seemed to know their way around a city considered by some a very wicked city indeed. They knew what to avoid—seamy neighborhoods, deserted streets at night, invitations from strangers—and what they could count on to be safe. When I was about their age, I shot my BB gun at a man's hat and hit it; and when I was fifteen, I had sex with my cousin in her bedroom in Woodmere, Long Island while her parents were at a funeral. I wondered what all the fuss was about, but Ella seemed to enjoy it very much. I suppose, this being the early nineteen twenties, I was somewhat before my time in the sex department. There was a small scare when Ella's period was late but it turned out to be a false alarm. God only knows what would have happened to Ella if she had got herself knocked up. A trip to Denmark to get it "taken care of"?

I also filched coins from my father's overcoat pocket from time to time as it hung in the downstairs closet—never more than twenty-five cents at a time—and bought pulp magazines like *Doc Savage* and *Black Cat* at the neighborhood cigar store. These were items that my father would not allow in the house, so I had to stuff them in my pants before I ran upstairs to my room. Phyllis and I rarely questioned our children the way a lot of nervous parents did. "Where were you?" "What were you doing yesterday afternoon?" "How did your dress get dirty?" and so on. So long as they were healthy, went to school every day, did their homework, and didn't seem to be hiding some awful secret, we let them more or less alone. Kate said she wanted to be a lawyer when she grew up, and Henry said there were no lady lawyers. Henry wanted to be a physicist like J. Robert Oppenheimer.

By this time Phyllis had gone back to work. It didn't surprise me to find out that she was quite good at her job, and although she started out as a volunteer, in a short while she was bringing home a weekly paycheck. Her boss, Arnie Brill, sounded a lot like my former boss, Fred Forstman, a voluble, curious autodidact. As she had threatened, she was home just about every night for dinner, during which she overflowed with stories about Arnie. Apparently, he was on some unspecified "list" which meant he might be called to testify at the McCarthy hearings in D.C. I knew several people in publishing or television or some aspect of show business, who were either vaguely or explicitly harassed by certain men in Washington who seemed—defying both good will and common sense—to think that movie actors and radio commentators and the like were active in a "red menace." Looking back, I didn't take the threats as seriously as I probably should have. Phyllis was a fervent ally of her boss. Together they had produced a couple of radio shows that satirized the irrationality of McCarthyites. I said, "Is that such a good idea?" Her answer was, "Is free speech a good idea?"

During one of our cocktail hours in late March, Phyllis, in her breathless mode, told me that Arnie Brill had been called to testify before the House Un-American Activities Committee—HUAC, an ugly sound.

"They're going to ask him if he ever was a member of the Party."

"And was he?" I asked.

"I think for a week or two in his early twenties. Everybody was."

"I wasn't."

"We're not talking about you," she said. "Those two shows we did last year apparently stepped on some very sensitive toes. I'm beginning to wish we hadn't done them.

No, I didn't mean that. I'm glad we did them. Somebody's got to speak up."

I asked her what Arnie had to worry about. It wasn't going to be a picnic but what exactly could they do to him?

Phyllis explained that it wasn't a question so much of what they could do to him, but what he would do when they asked him to "name names," meaning rat on his friends and former friends. They were diabolical that way; they wanted to make their witnesses squirm. "If he gives them the names of men who were with him in the Party he'll feel terribly guilty. If he refuses, they'll cite him for contempt. It's a no-win situation."

"What's he going to do?"

She didn't know. He was agonizing over this. I wondered what I would have done in the same circumstances. I didn't know either. I asked her if Arnie was sure he was going to be called. Pretty sure, she said. It was just a matter of time. "It's a terrible time," she said. "Ike doesn't want to do anything. Ike could say something but he just doesn't. He waits and sees how things are going to sort themselves out. That's not right, Walt, the president could stop this!"

"I'm not so sure," I said.

She told me I was just as bad as our passive president. Ike should be impeached, she went on. By this time she had reached the outer limits of common sense so I just shut up.

As I said to Barry, later that evening, "You can imagine Macbeth getting impeached, maybe, or Stalin, but Eisenhower? You might as well try to impeach Gandhi."

For the next few weeks Phyllis seemed distracted. She was coming home later and later and skipped a few dinners altogether. Kate complained that her mom was neglecting her and Henry. I must say it wasn't bad having dinner with the two of them without Phyllis' sharp comments.

I talked to Barry about the person I was now calling "the new Phyllis."

"I should think you'd be pleased. Now you can watch Ed Sullivan without her telling you that you're just a middlebrow. No, I forget myself, he's on Sunday. She's here on Sunday."

"I know I should be delighted," I said, wondering why I wasn't. Why should I care if she's more absent than present? Should I care? "I'm confused," I said.

"That's okay," Barry said. "It's nice to have choices, isn't it?"

KATE CAME home from school a few weeks later and went straight to bed. Barry was at home and reported that she looked "ghastly." He met me at the front door. "I think she needs to see a doctor."

"Where's Phyllis?"

"She's still at work," he said. "I tried calling her but she's in some meeting or something." He raised his eyebrows. "Grete's very worried."

Barry should have told the person on the phone that it was an emergency and pulled her out of her fucking meeting or whatever it was, but I didn't tell him this. I never wanted to argue with him. I took the stairs two at a time. Grete was standing near Kate's bed. "She's not good, Mr. Samson," she said. "She feels like she have a bad fever. I go now."

I thanked Grete and bent over my daughter. Her eyes were closed. She was under the covers but apparently had not removed her clothes, except for her shoes. Her bedside radio was on, but it had slipped out of its frequency and was emitting only static. I turned it off. I said her name. She didn't stir. Her face was flushed and blotchy and her hair had separated into damp strings. My knees went soft.

I said "Kate!"

Without opening her eyes she made a sound but it wasn't a word.

"What's the matter, honey?"

She touched her head. "Hurts."

I put my palm against her forehead. It burned. "You have a fever," I said. "I'm going to call the doctor."

Henry came to the door of Kate's room. "What's she got?"

"A headache. Did you just get home from school?"

Henry nodded and then said it wasn't like any headache he ever saw. More like she had been hit over the head by a hammer. I told him I could do without his comments, his sister was sick, couldn't he see that? Meanwhile I soundlessly cursed Phyllis for not doing her job as the mother. I was angry, scared out of my wits; I'd never seen anyone so young so stricken. The idea that she might die was so terrifying I found that I could hardly breathe. I told Kate I would be right back, though I'm pretty sure her ears were not transmitting, and called Phyllis' number at work. The girl on the other end said, "I'll see if I can locate her." "You damn well better locate her," I shouted, "and now, not in ten minutes, but right this minute! Schnell!" The shouting obviously did the trick: Phyllis was on the phone within a couple of minutes.

"What's the emergency, Walt. I was in an important meeting!"

"Kate's sick. She can't move. Come home. Right away."

"Call Dr. Cooper," she said.

"I put in a call."

Phyllis said she'd be right home. "I hope I can find a cab. Or can you send Barry to pick me up?"

This would involve a trip twice as long as a cab ride—assuming she could get one near her office below Wall Street. "I'll send him," I said.

As soon as I hung up Dr. Cooper called. "I'll be right over," he said. Instead of reassuring me, his urgency made me more anxious. I went back upstairs to wait for the doctor, who arrived at the house within an hour. He put his bag down on the floor and went into the bathroom to wash his hands. The only motion coming from Kate was her breathing, quick and shallow. He came back with a towel still between his hands. "Let's have a look at you," he said to the unresponsive Kate. Dr. Cooper was roughly my age, maybe a year or so older. He wore gray flannels and a muted tweed jacket, a uniform of sorts: Ivy League education, top medical school, almost limitless power over his young patients and their families. He didn't seem to get the point of the few jokes I had told him, so I had long ago stopped trying to make him smile or laugh. He was a good, thorough physician. We didn't call each other by our first names, though he had been seeing Kate and Henry since they were infants. The doctor sat down on Kate's bed and gently peeled back the covers to listen to her heart. Her eyelids fluttered. He asked her to open her mouth. He stuck a tongue depressor into it. She gagged and her eyes began to water. He asked her to touch her chin to her chest. She couldn't. I knew this to be a bad sign. Polio? He reached into his bag and pulled out a thermometer which he slipped between her lips. He wrapped his hand around her wrist and consulted his watch. Stillness took over. But my heart was beating so fiercely I was sure Dr. Cooper could hear it. After about three minutes, he removed the thermometer. "Well," he said, "It looks like she's running a slight fever."

I asked him how high it was.

"Just over a hundred and three," he said.

"What do we do now?" I said. "What do you think it is?"

Dr. Cooper looked at me as if I were a slow student. "Could be almost anything," he said, as he stowed his tools in the black bag and snapped it smartly shut. "I don't like to guess at this stage."

"It's serious though?"

The doctor avoided looking at my face, "As I said, it could be any of a number of things."

"Polio?"

"We can't count that out. I'd like to get this young lady into the hospital."

"You mean now?"

He answered with the tiniest trace of impatience in his voice. "It's the prudent thing to do. We'll run some tests. Now I don't want you to jump to any conclusions before we get the results. For all we know it may simply be a bad flu. There's a lot of that going around right now. Or mononucleosis."

Phyllis burst into the room, still wearing her coat, hat, and gloves. "Darling child! How are you?"

Henry, who was lurking in the doorway, said, "I don't think she can answer you, Mom." No one paid any attention to him.

The Samson family circle was complete, all of it in one small bedroom, the air filled with emotions swirling, most of all—except for the object of it—anxiety over the unidentified thing which had grabbed Kate by the throat. Phyllis sat down on the bed and stroked her daughter's cheek saying, "Poor baby girl, you'll feel better soon." She bent to kiss Kate's cheek. She kept murmuring to her poor baby girl, over and over again. Kate opened her eyes with what looked like a huge effort and smiled wanly. Did she know how sick she was?

I left the room with Dr. Cooper—what *was* his first name anyway?—and walked him down to the front door where Barry was holding his coat and hat. I thanked the doctor who said he would be waiting for us at New York Hospital. "Please get her there as quickly as you can." Everything he said to me intensified my anxiety.

I think I must have gone into some kind of emotional overdrive. Phyllis and I managed to get Kate out of bed and to her feet, where she wobbled back and forth. Phyllis put a bathrobe over her shoulders. She whimpered. "Oh oh, my head . . ."

"We're taking you to the hospital, darling," Phyllis said. "You'll feel better in no time."

"Throw up," said Kate and she did, down the front of her clothes and robe, moist, green vomit. She stood there, trying, I think, to understand what was happening to her.

Henry said "Yuk."

Phyllis yelled at him to go get his robe for Kate. "You're a heartless boy," she said. "Do what I say! Now!" Henry fled.

Barry was ready with the car. He had turned on the motor. He looked grave. Leaving Henry behind, Phyllis and I climbed into the backseat with Kate between us. Her eyes were closed, her head lolled against the back of the seat. She gave off heat you could feel down your side. I asked Phyllis what she thought it was.

"Hush," she said. "Kate can hear us."

Barry was driving a lot faster than he usually did.

Phyllis said, "Dr. Cooper should have called an ambulance."

For the first time ever, Barry spoke to her from the driver's seat. "This is a lot quicker, ma'am. I can get you there in less than ten minutes."

My mouth had gone so dry I couldn't speak. I looked at Kate, who seemed to be drifting off somewhere we might not be able to retrieve her from. The idea that she might die was monstrous but real, as if you had been told that an object in outer space was heading straight for our planet. You believe it, you can't believe it, you believe it. The heat from Kate's body penetrated my coat, my suit, and my heart. I held her limp, moist, hot hand and, although I had no faith in God or at this moment in anything else I prayed. *Please don't let Kate die. I'll do anything if you'll keep her alive, anything, even give up Barry.*

We arrived at the emergency entrance of the hospital in less than ten minutes. I jumped out of the backseat—no eye exchange with Barry, no wasted motions—and reached back into the car to help Kate. She couldn't stand so I picked her up in my arms and carried her through the front door, which Barry held open for us. Dr. Cooper, in a crisp white coat, was waiting for us beside a rolling gurney and a young man to push it. Cooper told me to put Kate on the gurney. Phyllis tried to help but there was nothing for her to help with, so she just fluttered and talked to Kate in a soft, pleading voice. As soon as Kate was safely aboard, the young man started to steer her off down the hall. Dr. Cooper said, "Why don't you two have a seat in the waiting room?" He pointed. "I'll come out and get you when she's finished."

I thought, *finished what? Doesn't he mean until he's finished?* Things were not making sense.

Phyllis said, "Hold me." I spread my arms and took her body between them. She made a gasping sound and let her head fall against my chest. I told her everything was going to be all right, aware of how fatuous this sounded, but what else could I say?

Phyllis said something.

"What did you say?"

"I said, what if she dies?"

"She isn't going to die."

"How do you know? You don't know."

I repeated what I'd told her. This seemed to upset her and she pulled away. Where was Barry? I wanted him to hold me the way I had held Phyllis. I wasn't strong enough.

"It's the not being able to help her," Phyllis said.

I nodded. I asked her if she would like some coffee. She shook her head. We sat down in the waiting room. There were others waiting, whose presence I felt rather than saw. I was aware of shuffling and sighing. A child was asking his parent the same thing over and over again without apparently getting any answer. It was far too hot, and the air was choking with disinfectant that irritated my nose. Every so often ghosts slipped by in the hall. I told Phyllis I was going to get some air and please to fetch me if Dr. Cooper came back. "I'll be right by the front door."

Barry had the car parked smartly against the curb a few feet from the door. I looked in: He was asleep, his head just barely down on his chest. I knocked on the window. He looked up: "How is Kate?"

I told him we didn't know anything yet. "They took her off somewhere. Why don't you go home? We'll probably be here all night." Barry refused, saying he'd rather wait. I reached inside the car and caressed his head. This simple gesture aroused me and I was ashamed; I didn't want Barry to know. I was a flawed man, a worthless person, an animal. I thanked him, and assured him I'd let him know about Kate as soon as we did. Then I went back to the waiting room.

Phyllis was sitting rigidly in her plastic seat. A magazine lay on her lap, unread. I sat down next to her and said, "This is truly awful. I wish we could do something."

"We wait," she said. You couldn't help admire her grit.

"Mr. Samson?"

The man the voice belonged to stood directly in front of me, where I had fallen asleep sitting upright. I opened my eyes and saw Dr. Cooper's buttons eyeing me. Phyllis was on her feet.

"You can see your daughter now," the doctor said.

I asked him what was wrong with her.

They had drawn spinal fluid he told us, and found that it was, as he had suspected, meningitis. "It's the more severe manifestation of the disease, but there's a happy side to it; we now have antibiotic medicine, chiefly penicillin, to target the bacteria. It usually does the trick." He made it sound as if he were adding salt to something tasteless. "I'm not going to pretend for your sake that this isn't a very serious illness. Before the war, she might not have pulled through. But these miracle drugs . . ." He moved his head up and down to indicate, I suppose, that modern medicine was miraculous. They would have to keep her in the hospital at least a week. He went on to say he would inform Kate's school, for this was highly contagious.

Phyllis said, "You said we could see Kate."

"Yes. She's sleeping," Dr. Cooper said. "She's had a somewhat rough night. I suggest you take just a peek at her, not try to wake her."

"Is she going to be okay?" I asked. The three of us stood stiffly outside Kate's private room. My left hand, inside the pocket of my trousers, played with my keys.

"Well," he said, "In a relatively few cases there's some impairment, because of the infection you see, in the brain. A slight hearing loss, some cognitive difficulties." He was reciting, as if he had memorized the textbook. Abruptly, he pulled himself back. "But we don't have to think about that now. That probably won't happen." I looked at Phyllis glaring at Dr. Cooper, who seemed unable to say anything unambiguous. "Aside from this, she should have a complete recovery. But it will take some time. She'll have to stay home from school for a couple of weeks. Regain her strength."

I had no idea what time it was. The corridor was lit, but for all I knew it could have been ten or one A.M. or six in the morning. I looked at my watch: two-thirty. What had happened in the hours since we brought Kate to the hospital? I was tired, my body screamed tired, my head was heavy on my neck. I think I stank of perspiration. The doctor opened the door to Kate's room. It took a moment before my eyes could make her out on the bed. Kate lay on her back, one pillow beneath her head. An IV dripped something into her left arm. A nurse sat on the room's only chair with some knitting in her hands. She looked up and nodded at us. She began to get up. But Dr. Cooper told her, "Please don't get up. You just stay right there." To us: "I've asked for a special nurse to come in and sit with her for the next couple of nights. I assume you don't object," Dr. Cooper said.

Phyllis began to cry.

"She's going to get better," Dr. Cooper said. "I wouldn't lie to you. I have every expectation that the antibiotic will do the trick."

Phyllis approached the bed. She said Kate's name softly. There was no response.

Dr. Cooper said they had given Kate a painkiller to blunt the pain of the spinal tap. She wasn't likely to wake up until daylight, if then. He suggested we go home and get some rest. Phyllis protested saying she wanted to spend the night in Kate's room. The doctor wasn't happy about this, but Phyllis dug in her heels and finally Cooper backed down. "I'll see if I can have a cot brought in for you. This goes against my better judgment."

"Why?" Phyllis said. She pulled off her hat and went to hang her coat in the tiny closet. "Mothers want to be with their sick children," she said. "It should be normal procedure."

Dr. Cooper caught my eye and sent me a message that said something like, *God protect me from hysterical women*. I wouldn't play ball with him; I thought Phyllis' point was extremely well taken.

"As long as you're here," I said to Phyllis, "I think I'll go home for a few hours. I'll be back first thing in the morning."

Barry was an angel. He listened for several minutes without commenting as I talked about how Kate's illness was my punishment for leading a wicked and decadent life.

Then he said, "And why is Kate getting punished? She's the one who's sick, not you. What did *she* do to deserve this? Honestly, Walt, why are you bringing this back to yourself? I mean look, your daughter has this terrible disease and all you can think about is what did *I* do. You didn't do anything, this has nothing to do with you."

"I'm sorry I said that. I shouldn't have said that. I shouldn't even have thought it. What's the matter with me?" What he said to me was as stunning and painful as a bullet in the chest. I could hardly breathe.

"She's going to be okay—right? Why are you beating yourself up?"

⌒

THEY KEPT Kate in the hospital just under two weeks, antibiotics dripped into her arm for days on end. I left work early during this time, bringing some work with me in the event that she was sleeping. At first she was too groggy to recognize me. But after a couple of days she managed to say "hi" in a weak little voice and try to smile. Every couple of hours a nurse came in to take her temperature and blood pressure, and ask her a few simple questions like who's the president of the U.S. of A. And what month comes after June and what was her middle name. Various friends, including Fred Forstman, ailing himself, had sent flowers and get-well messages. The flowers stood in chunky glass vases on the dresser and windowsill, some of the flowers drooping. An enormous, rococo bouquet was delivered from a Madison Avenue florist with a sweet note from Mary and Edgar Fleming. Charlie McCann sent a tin of chocolates from Sherry's.

I watched for signs of mental difficulties or hearing loss and was much relieved not to find any. Phyllis came every day and we often sat together and talked quietly while our daughter slept. I'd read that a child's sickness frequently drives parents apart. In our case it was just the opposite. For once, both of us seemed to be focused on something other than ourselves. I guess Barry's remark to me in the car had a salutary effect, and I no longer viewed Kate's illness as my own personal punishment—except for the times I slipped back and beat myself up.

But while Kate continued to recover without apparent setback, I was profoundly shaken by nearly losing her. I couldn't imagine anything more terrible than your child's death, not even running someone over in the street, or seeing your lover shot. I know I would have given my own life to save hers. I was so shaken that for months after she came home from the hospital I woke up around three in the morning, trembling and covered with sweat. It was as if the notion of mortality had passed me by until Kate fell sick. Where had I been? What had I been thinking? I had been complacent and stupid. Abruptly, everything shifted and I found myself in a constant state of anxiety. I tried to shake free of it but, like your shadow on a sunny day, it followed me everywhere. Sometimes I thought that if I escaped my present life and disappeared into another place, like a Mexican seaside village—bringing Barry along with me, of course—the anxiety would disappear as well. I tried hard to hide the chaos and I think I did pretty well at this, but Barry noticed something. "You're awfully jumpy these days." I determined not to let him see how upset I was.

While Kate recuperated at home, I left work early to sit with her each afternoon. A classmate who lived nearby brought her homework so she wouldn't fall too far behind in her studies. She had lost some weight and her cheeks were sallow, but you could tell her health was improving because she was restless and kept asking when she could go back to school.

On the fifth day of this I said, "Henry tells me you have a boyfriend."

Kate flushed. "I do not have a boyfriend. Henry's a liar."

"Well," I said, "I guess maybe I got it wrong." I was pretty sure I hadn't got it wrong. Though Henry was something of a snitch, lying wasn't one of his strong suits. He loved his sister but I guess he couldn't help being envious of her pale beauty and her popularity at school. Smart children like Henry, especially if they don't look like young

Adonises and aren't good athletes, have a serious disadvantage at school.

"Henry doesn't know anything about me."

"I wouldn't be too sure about that," I said.

"And where was I supposed to have met this so-called boyfriend?"

"At a dance at Trinity last fall."

"I'm going to get him!" This was a steely side of my daughter that seemed to have emerged since her illness.

I told her having a boyfriend was nothing to be ashamed of. "You're certainly old enough to be the apple of some boy's eye."

In a tone I'd never heard her use before, she asked me if we could drop the subject. She opened a math book and took up a pencil and a pad of paper.

"I can take a hint," I said.

"Besides," she said, just as I was about to leave the room, "you've got a boyfriend. Why shouldn't I?"

CHAPTER 7

The movie camera lovingly memorializes in slow motion that moment when the wrecker's ball, after drawing slightly back, hurls itself against the brick wall, smashing into it, collapsing the wall and sending a huge veil of dust and rubble into the air.

After Kate confronted me in that minatory way, the ball hit me square in the chest, taking away my breath. I looked at her steadily and saw she wasn't kidding. Amazingly (because I was so stunned), I still considered my options. One: pretend I didn't hear what she had just said. Two: ask her to explain herself, and perhaps put her on the defensive. Three: act as if she were joking and say something like, "Well, doesn't that just put us in the same boat?" None of these options was especially attractive. I looked at her intently the way you might look at a tiger in the zoo—an apt image except that there were no bars between us; we were equals.

Kate looked back boldly; there was no mistaking what her eyes said: *I know about you and Barry.*

But instead of making her move, Kate retreated, just why, I'm not sure. Maybe she wanted to keep me twisting there. "I've got to finish this math, Dad," she said, as if nothing at all had taken place. "I'll talk to you later."

And all this time I had been worried that Grete or Marie would discover my secret, and that one of them would shake me down to keep quiet about it. I should have been worried about my own beloved daughter. She might tell anyone. It was inconceivable that a fifteen-year-old girl could keep a secret as provocative as this one. I shouldn't expect that she would be able to. Who would she tell? Her mother.

I left the room trying not to let my distress show. I walked downstairs like a man in his dotage, light-headed with anxiety, slow and tentative, each step seeming to punctuate the precariousness of my situation. Ten minutes earlier I had been a relatively free man, now I was trapped. I felt almost heedless, the reality of the situation giving me another opportunity to make changes. I went down to my study, shut the door and sat down at my desk. There was a bottle of Scotch handy. From this I poured myself several fingers and swallowed it down in a gulp. I was grateful how much and how quickly this helped.

I told myself that although I acted irrationally from time to time, I was as capable as the next educated man to employ reason. I considered: suppose Kate told her mother what she had accused me of. Phyllis might not believe her, denial being the powerful state of mind that it is. Ask the daughter what makes her think so. The daughter can't come up with evidence that counts with the mother. The mother dismisses the daughter as a fantasist. The daughter slinks off. Or, what if the mother believes the daughter? Justifiably angry, she asks me to "please leave my house." That would remove one choice, with only one left: to leave. With Barry, of course—if he would come with me. We could move somewhere like San Francisco or Province-town or Key West. Was this rational? Who could tell until afterwards—and then it would be too late.

But would I leave? Strong as my longing was to live openly with Barry, I couldn't see myself giving up my job, my family—especially my two dear children—my creature comforts like membership in the Orange Club. For what? For sex, maybe once a day, if that, for twenty minutes with a man who might, at any moment, decide he's had enough of a middle-aged, middle-class jerk? I was fairly sure that I would lose my job if the "scandal" was hinted at in that smarmy way of theirs by Leonard Lyons or Winchell in their gossip columns. Even though publishing was a refuge for assorted oddballs—alcoholics, oversexed men and women, and the effetes who kept their sexual preferences hidden from the outside world—and pretty much anything went so long as you delivered what you were paid to deliver, going public was a line one did not cross without consequences. Still, publishing wasn't *life*, it was but a tiny, musty corner in a great big house. Nobody but those plying its trade gave a shit. You asked someone the title of a book they recommended to you and they could tell you. They might actually know the author's name as well. But ask them who published it and they would go blank.

If I ran away with a young man, I couldn't expect to be forgiven by most of my old friends, classmates, acquaintances, wife, or children. Outcast! Was I basically weak or strong because I was reluctant to pull away from all things large and small that gave me my equilibrium? It mattered—I wanted to be strong. Didn't it take more guts to stay, stick it out with my family?

I realized, after pouring myself a second Scotch, that I had a pounding headache.

Thinking about our little encounter later, I began to realize that Kate, rather than going straight to her mother, meant to keep our secret between the two of us. I wish I could articulate just how I knew this. There was something so controlled, so controlling about the way she looked at me; the look seemed to seal a pact.

Hoping to extinguish my headache, I took two aspirin and waited for the pain to dissolve. My life had never before seemed quite so fractured. And not lost on me but underscored heavily was the fact that this was all my fault; I was architect and engineer. I couldn't blame anyone else, couldn't blame fate, couldn't blame God, couldn't blame my parents.

⚓

THE FOLLOWING day I went to B. Altman's on Thirty-Fourth Street and bought an oval aquamarine in an antique setting and a thin golden chain from which to hang it. It wasn't all that expensive but it looked smart—classy but not showy. I thought it would suit Kate. I had it gift-wrapped, and as she handed me the package the saleslady told me that someone was a very lucky person. I thanked her.

As soon as I got home I went straight to Kate's room. She was sitting up in bed, wearing a sweater and plaid skirt. The color had returned to her cheeks and her hair was brushed so that it shone. I said, "You must be feeling a lot better."

"I can't stand being sick anymore. I got dressed. Mom says I can go back to school next week. Why can't I go tomorrow?"

"I guess your mother asked Dr. Cooper," I said. "We have to go by his orders. Here." I handed her the box in its wrapping, which she immediately tore off. She opened the box, "What's this?" she said.

"A little something to let you know how much you mean to us, how precious you are. You realize that we almost lost you."

"Does Mom know you bought me this?"

"I haven't had a chance to tell her yet. I saw it in the store window and I couldn't resist getting it for you. Don't you like it?"

"Yeah, sure I like it." She still had it in her palm and was looking at it as if it might have something to say to her.

Then she hopped off the bed and sat down at her vanity table, where she put the chain around her neck and fastened it. "How do I look?"

I told her the stone matched her eyes. She grinned.

All the while we were both aware of the thing neither of us would talk about. It lay there, a nasty beast hiding in the back of the closet, biding its time before springing out. Kate thanked me again, but didn't move from where she was staring at herself in the triptych mirror.

"I'm glad you like it."

"You didn't have to do that," she said.

"I know that. Of course I didn't have to. I *wanted* to. There's the difference."

This conversation had stalled. I told her I'd see her at dinner. "That is, if you're well enough to come downstairs."

Phyllis came home a few minutes later. By this time I was sitting in my study reading a manuscript about peacetime uses of nuclear energy. The agent's covering letter had stressed that this was an important subject, that the author, a retired admiral, earned his chops, and that I would be extremely foolish to give this book a pass. "I'm sending it to you first off," the agent wrote. My eyes glazed; I just couldn't get it up for nuclear power, however "important" it was to the future of mankind. I viewed my distraction as ominous. *This is your job! Do it. Do it with joy.* I wondered where Barry was.

Phyllis burst into the room. She ripped off her hat, sending a pin flying. She talked excitedly. "Arnie has to testify," she said. "It's the worst thing that could possibly happen. How can they do that to this lovely man?"

"But you've known for a while this was going to happen. Why are you so surprised?" I was giving her a hard time when I should have tried to make her feel better. She seemed to ignore my remark and insisted that Arnie wasn't ready to testify.

"I doubt one is ever ready for this sort of inquisition," I said. I sounded inexcusably smug. I kept wondering where Barry was.

"If he doesn't rat on his erstwhile friends he goes to jail for contempt."

"It's a lousy time," I said.

She asked me if that was all I had to say. We knew how to get under each other's skin; it was amazingly easy. Did that mean we were truly devoted to each other or the opposite? Who knew?

"You're no help," she said. "I'm going to go up and see Kate. Have you been up to see her?"

"Wait," I said. "Before you go up. I bought her a little present. I think she's wearing it."

"Walter—how sweet of you." She started to melt before my eyes. "I hope Henry won't be too envious."

"When he recovers from meningitis, I'll give him something too," I said. Completely uncalled for.

Barry came into my study a few minutes later, probably having waited until he heard Phyllis go upstairs. I asked him where he'd been. "Gassing up Baby," he said. I didn't altogether believe him even though there was no evidence that he was lying. He asked me if he could bum a cigarette, he was all out of Camels. Paranoia crawled along the skin of my arms. "You're usually here when I get home," I said.

"Not this time," he said, accepting the cigarette I handed him without lingering for a friendly squeeze of the hand or something more. I told him Kate knew about him, that is, him and me. He said he figured it was only a matter of time. He sighed. "And I was just getting used to living here," he said.

"Barry, this is serious!"

"I know it is, man, but a little humor never hurt any situation." He tried to reassure me; Kate wouldn't tell anyone. He knew her pretty well. She adored me, she wouldn't betray me. I answered that she also loved her mother; if she kept quiet she would be betraying her mother. If she told her mother I would be the one betrayed. Kate was in an awkward place. I didn't envy her. "You can see how she's being pulled in opposite directions," I told him.

Barry went right on, as if nothing I'd said made the slightest difference, concluding—and I must admit it made sense—that Kate would hardly light the fuse on the bomb that would explode the family. "She likes things the way they are."

Barry picked up the glass I had been drinking from and took a couple of swallows. His Adam's apple bobbed up and down. I wanted to lick it. Distracted by my own lust I hardly listened as Barry went on to complain that I hadn't been myself since Kate's illness. I knew that already, he didn't have to tell me. "Don't go nutty on me," he said. I felt a tear leave my eye and roll down my cheek. "Jesus," Barry said. "You're in rotten shape."

At that moment we heard Phyllis coming down the stairs. Barry swiftly withdrew to the servants' part of the house. I composed myself as best I could, picked up the manuscript and waited for my wife to come in.

"It's beautiful, Walt. I mean it, it's perfectly lovely. What a nice father you are."

Her admiration for me was so patent that I was certain Kate had said nothing to incriminate me. But Phyllis was worried. Kate had begun to cry, and when Phyllis asked her what was the matter, Kate said she didn't know, she didn't know why she was crying.

❦

THE FOLLOWING day, Arnie Brill, Phyllis' boss, dove from an eleventh storey window—a bathroom—in the federal courthouse on Foley Square, landing on a car, injuring its driver, and killing himself.

Phyllis found out about it while she was at work. She called me right away. I could barely understand what she was telling me because her voice was muffled by her tears.

She said her office was in turmoil. I had met Arnie once, briefly, and found him less than impressive; there was something furtive about his face, his eyes, that stuck with me. Still I was angry this had happened. What kind of country were we living in? Where was our brave soldier-president when we needed him?

"Did he have a family?"

"There's a wife in Wilkes-Barre. They're separated. Their two kids live with her."

"A silver lining of sorts," I said. I could almost see her scowling.

We both hung up. When I saw her next, she looked as if she had been disassembled and put back together wrong. Her hair was all over the place, her slip hung beneath the hem of her skirt. It made you wonder what she had been doing. Barry, who had fetched her in the car, came into the study with her and said, "Mr. Samson, I brought Mrs. Samson home. I don't think she's feeling very well."

"Thank you, Barry, I'm grateful to you for taking such good care of my wife."

"Thank you, Mr. Samson."

Phyllis took out a handkerchief and wiped her eyes. "Oh Walter, what have we done?"

"Who?"

"Those monsters in Washington. They're not human. Why can't they leave people alone?"

"Come here, Phyll." I held out my arms. I'm not a complete bastard; I can be reached. Phyllis fell against me and held on tight. She was perspiring; the smell rising off her body stung my nose. It made me pity her. I held my breath.

Because Arnie was Jewish, the funeral was scheduled for the following day. Phyllis said I shouldn't go. Wouldn't it look odd, I asked her, my not going to the funeral with her? She said we were in the second half of the twentieth century, wives did things alone. "You have your work," she said. The entire staff of WNYC would be there, as well as his family and friends, even the separated wife. I needn't go. To be honest, I was relieved because I hate funerals. This hardly put me in a class of one, but I found them too fantastic. Years earlier I had gone to the funeral of one of my father's cousins and didn't recognize the man the eulogizers were talking about, so heavily did they apply the brush of fiction to a man no one loved and most people feared. So I was delighted that Phyllis urged me to go to work instead.

The papers headlined Arnie's suicide; no one called it an accident. Depending on the publisher's political stance, the story either praised the House Un-American Activities Committee for rooting out yet another disloyal citizen, or else condemned our indigenous fascism "capable of hounding a decent, innocent man to his premature death." I wasn't surprised at how Arnie's suicide divided sentiments. Some people thought Abraham Lincoln was an opportunist and a hypocrite. Some people believed Hitler was a savior.

It took longer for Phyllis to shake off her grief over Arnie's death than it had taken Kate to recover from meningitis. Often, when I came home, I would find the two of them in our bedroom enveloped by an air of intimacy. Phyllis would be lying on her bed, with a box of Kleenex on the bedside table, her eyes often puffy and red, Kate half-sitting, half-reclining in her mother's chaise lounge. I knew as soon as I entered the room that they had been talking about something they didn't want me to hear. Their words had flown off and were lost. *I caught them in my inner ear.*

You know your father loves you.

Yes, I know he does.

He's used to having his own way. His mother spoiled him. She called him "my little prince."

"What's so bad about that?"

"It tends to make a man feel he's better than anyone else."

"Why did you marry Dad?"

"What a question! Because I loved him."

"Even though he acts like he thinks he's a prince?"

"He doesn't do that all the time. Look at how he came home every day early just to be with you when you were sick."

"I know."

"Get me a cigarette, will you? They're over there."

"Mom, are all men like Dad?"

"I wouldn't know. Most of them, I guess. We women have to put up with a lot of crap. Excuse me for that. But we get a lot, don't we?"

"Do you still love him the way you did when you got married?"

"Enough questions, Kate. Have you done your homework?"

"I love you, Mom."

The several times I walked in on this pas de deux, I withdrew, after taking off my jacket and exchanging it for my favorite cashmere cardigan. They stopped talking and stared at me until I had left the room. It was unnerving. Kate was always wearing the pendant; I figured she wore it to bed.

It didn't occur to me to find anything unusual about Phyllis' prolonged sorrow. I knew she had liked and admired her boss a lot. I was also aware of how theatrical her responses tended to be—about almost everything.

DEATH WAS multiplying around us that spring. Fred Forstman finally gave up the ghost and was dispatched with a large and star-studded funeral at Temple Emanu-El on Fifth Avenue, a synagogue so assimilated that wearing a yarmulke was frowned upon, if not prohibited. Attendees included the mayor of New York with his wife, embraced by a mink stole, the heads of NBC and CBS, and a couple of aging movie stars whose memoirs Forstman had brought out with the help of ghosts. I had to go to this funeral, there was no way I could escape; and to be perfectly honest, I wanted to see how they managed to get rid of all the wrinkles and carbuncles on this man, the very things that made him singular, and in some ways—maybe perverse—beloved. The rabbi sounded like Anthony Eden and looked like my dentist, Dr. Leonard. The speeches lasted nearly an hour, with the temperature in the building rising a degree or two every fifteen minutes or so. By the end it was stifling.

Two Forstman sons gave us a look at Fred at home. Was this the bawdy teller of tall tales, misogynistic individual I had learned to love? "He took us on picnics to Bear Mountain." "He made funny hats for us to wear at birthday parties." "He loved *Pinocchio*; he saw it ten times." A former colleague at the milk company where he had worked years before coming to Griffin extolled him as a "gentleman's gentleman" and no one sniggered. His wife said nothing but sat in the front pew throughout, wiping her eyes. The rabbi talked about the generosity of his spirit matched only by the generosity of his purse. That didn't sound quite right to me, but never mind.

I told Barry about the funeral. He said he wished he had been there. "Our memories are mostly separate," he said. "Do you realize that? We almost never do anything together just the two of us except when I'm driving you someplace."

A month or so after the stir created by Forstman's death, everyone at the publishing house had slipped back into their daily routines. It was then brought to the attention of upper management that Griffin House had a small but worrisome cash flow problem. This news reached us in the form of a memo, "for internal distribution only," from the publisher. The problem had arisen mainly because, in an effort to beat out the competition, we had got into the habit of shelling out bloated advances to authors who either never delivered as promised or whose books had disappointing sales. There was the book by a doctor, for example, that promised eternal life in return for foregoing all foods beginning with the letter C. This is an exaggeration, but not so farfetched as one might think. Diet books by the pound. One advocated eating only grapefruit, presumably until you practically dropped dead from malnutrition. Another that you could eat anything you wanted, except that no portion was allowed to be any larger than what you would feed a hamster. Yet another instructed you to make love three times a day for six weeks. Another killer. None of these books earned back their advances, although the sex one came close. There was a surgeon from a celebrated clinic who promised a book that would extend a person's life by a good two-and-a-half years if he would adhere to a regimen that eschewed all protein, fat, and all citrus fruits. The doctor's book was three years past deadline, and I called him many times only to be told that "the doctor is in surgery" and would call me back. He never did. We didn't go after people like him, we simply wrote it off as you do a bad debt.

One night I had an especially vivid dream about a silent movie star, someone like Theda Bara or Gloria Swanson, dark shining hair, wide round eyes heavily outlined with kohl, bending over a cradle and covering the baby lying in it with great, slurpy kisses. The dream stayed with me through breakfast, came with me in the car, and abruptly turned into an idea for a book, as we approached Sixty-Seventh Street. I tried the idea on Barry. I treasured these times when he and I were in the car together. No one could interrupt; no one could hear what we were saying to each other. We were sealed together inside a capsule. Taking a risk, I sat in front with him. Sometimes I put my left hand on his right thigh. He would frown and accuse me of distracting him. "Do you want me to get into an accident?"

I asked him if he remembered a silent screen actress named Lucille Baroney, also known as Lula. He'd heard the name but nothing visual came to mind. I told him she was almost as popular as Lillian Gish and Mary Pickford. She wasn't much of an actress but she had a great body and could cry on demand, which made her a hot property. There was a lot of waterworks in silent movies. She was rumored to have had torrid romances with Charlie Chaplin, Douglas Fairbanks, Lionel Barrymore, and the Prince of Wales. Barry asked how old she was now. I guessed late sixties.

"A cow put out to pasture? What happens to all these old has-beens?"

"Would you read a memoir by her?"

"Probably, if it was juicy enough."

"I can't imagine it wouldn't be." I was thinking that if I bought another graceful mid-list book, it would sell fewer than five thousand copies and put Griffin that much further behind. I wished Forstman were still around to advise me; the man had an uncanny sense of what would sell and what wouldn't. I needed a moneymaker. "I seem to recall that Miss Lula or whatever her name was, enjoyed a varied sex life."

"You mean like you and me?"

Barry and I shared a quiet moment or two musing about this. Then we were at my office building. It was already almost nine-thirty and a few stragglers were entering the building in a hurry. I gave Barry's thigh a hasty squeeze and joined the latecomers.

I went straight to our so-called library where we kept reference books, *Who's Who*, *The World Almanac*, assorted dictionaries and encyclopedias, histories of English and American literature, and an encyclopedia of Hollywood from the birth of movies to the present. In this volume I found exactly what I was looking for.

I went back to my office, taking the book with me, and called Charlie McCann. "Hey pal, I need your help."

No one had ever said or suggested that Charlie wasn't a decent man; he was a grown-up boy scout without the fervor. It would never have occurred to me that he would do anything underhanded or break a promise or lie in order to make himself look better. This probably caused problems for him; most of us get through by resorting to one small subterfuge after another that we convince ourselves won't hurt anyone. But neither was Charlie too good to be true, because as I said earlier, part of him had been shut down during the war when he was sure he was going to die. He was married and had two young children to whom he was extremely kind. I would guess that his wife, Marcia, had to put up with unexplained periods of silence from her husband, which all in all, is not too high a price to pay for a good man. Charlie had reached a stage in his life where envy and resentment had said goodbye to him forever. That was a plus for me, because, had things been just a little different, he would have had my job and I his.

I asked Charlie to sit down. He was wearing the uniform—pink shirt, black string tie, dark gray trousers, neatly pressed, a muted Harris Tweed jacket with little twigs embedded in the cloth, and a good shave. He was a good-looking guy with a nose that had been smashed in a high school football game, giving him the look of an intelligent bruiser.

I told Charlie I wanted him to go after a memoir by Lucille Baroney.

"That old crock?" he said. "You must be joking."

I assured him I wasn't joking. "I think she lives somewhere near Boston."

"You say you got this idea from a dream?"

"Well, I probably shouldn't have told you that. It makes me sound like a lunatic."

"I'll buy that," he said. He pulled a pack of Chesterfields from his jacket pocket and lit up. There was no mistaking his feelings: he didn't like the idea. He considered himself to be a literary editor and so far had managed to stay away from the kind of book that Lucille Baroney's book would inevitably turn out to be: a series of anecdotes bordering on the sleazy. Charlie asked me if I though Griffin was really that sort of publisher.

"You betcha," I said. "Where have you been, my friend?"

Charlie sagged. He let out a deep sigh. "I suppose you're right," he said.

"Come on now," I said. "It's not so bad. Just think of her as one of those little folks from outer space, like that business in New Mexico. Little men with funny heads."

"It might not be worse than The Folly," he said, using the word we had attached to an epic battle with a Princeton historian who insisted that not a single word of his manuscript about the opening days of the Civil War be changed, even though it was crammed with inconsistencies and factual errors. It all ended with our not publishing the book and the author threatening to sue; the case was still pending.

I asked Charlie to talk with Lula Baroney. It would probably mean a trip to see her in her own house; she wasn't likely to want to come to New York to talk. We'd put him up in a nice Boston hotel like the Copley Plaza, give him an expense account. He could take in a Red Sox game.

He told me his daughter was in a play at school he had promised to see.

My skin began to prickle. He was making it hard for me to insist he follow through on this possibly madcap idea of mine. But I was the boss; it wasn't his decision. "I'm sorry . . ." I began and he interrupted me: "I shouldn't have said that. I can see Connie anytime. She always gets the leads in the play."

I thanked him. I really meant it. I counted on his steadiness and common sense—a commodity that seemed to me to be going dry in the general population. Take, for instance, the sticking power of Dianetics, dreamed up by a con artist named L. Ron Hubbard—the name was enough to get your doubts in gear. Many actually believed this man who claimed to be able to regress anyone to their pre-birth condition and thereby rid them of their hang-ups. Some people relegated Dianetics to the same category as psycho-analysis, which also smelled a little fishy. In any case, I counted heavily on Charlie to be where I needed him.

After consulting with our publisher, I gave Charlie an open-ended expense account, told him to spend as many days as he thought necessary. Take taxis, eat at Locke-Ober's, think of this as a working vacation. Some might think the task I was handing him would be a lark, but not Charlie, nor I, for that matter. To say it was soul-robbing would be to exaggerate, but it was heading in that direction. Charlie had studied English Literature at Harvard, was one of its stars, and had published a piece about a Donne elegy while still an undergraduate. The difference between Donne and Baroney was the difference between a filet mignon and a hot dog.

"Take a few days, don't be in too much of a hurry," I added as we both headed toward the door of my office. "Get to know the lady, don't promise her too much money, you know what I mean; I don't have to spell it out for you. We're going to have to hire a ghost to work with her, and good ghosts don't come cheap, as you know."

I told him to phone me whenever he felt like it. "I'm on call."

"You act like I'm going to Antarctica, for crissake," he said.

⤳

IT WAS remarkable how this new venture distracted me from my troubles—real and imagined—at home. Charlie stayed in touch. In fact, he wrote me daily letters on Copley Plaza stationery. I enjoyed these communications because they were so obviously meant to be read and appreciated by a connoisseur. It had been easy enough to locate and get an invitation to visit the lady in a triple-decker in the unlovely suburb of Somerville—"the second most heavily populated urban area in the United States. Most of the inhabitants live in three-storey wooden houses, one family per floor. The houses look like tinder boxes. Nobody puts a number on their house. What are they afraid of?" He had finally located Baroney's house by asking several neighbors who gave him a funny look; they were not used to strangers. The lady was waiting for him. She had dressed herself up in a gown that Charlie figured she had taken away with her when she finished one of her movies. "It was covered with those little disks that sparkle. It was ten-thirty in the morning." Even though Baroney had taken the hook that had "memoirs" as bait, she was suspicious to begin with; Charlie surmised suspicion was part of her nature or maybe she had been thrown this hook before without resolution. The place was "darker than a cat's asshole," he wrote, speculating that darkness is kinder than light to the ravages of age. "I groped my way onto the living room couch, bumping into a table on the way." Baroney asked him to excuse the mess. "There wasn't any. After sitting me down and plying me with coffee, she asked my name for the third time. 'I'll call you Charles if you don't mind,' she said. 'I loathe nicknames. And I want you to call me Lucille, never Lula. I loathe that name. It was probably that bitch, Hedda Hopper, who gave it to me. Made me sound like a common streetwalker.' "

Charlie was sure her manner of speaking came from an acting coach rather than her parents. But that was explainable; she came from the era when actors were taught to talk like English gentry, even though she only played in two or three "talkies" before she retired to a life of disappointed dreams. The woman's suspicion gradually melted into a river of life story. "It would have sounded tragic if it hadn't had so many horrible things in it: incest, alcoholism, a child born with missing fingers." She seemed to enjoy telling this story of tragedy compounded. Charlie admitted that he doubted a good deal of it—"too dramatic; there isn't time in one life for all that crap." Every once in a while he heard noises overhead, and it turned out that Lula's daughter lived on the second floor. "And when I said that I'd like to meet Claire," she said, 'No, you wouldn't—believe me,' which only piqued my curiosity. Just before I got up to leave I told Lula again that she had had a fascinating life and that we at Griffin House, a major book publisher, would like to bring out her memoirs." She said she'd think about it. 'Come back tomorrow.' It had the ring of a fairy tale where the hero has to do something three times in order to break the spell or get the girl or find the treasure."

The next day I received a second letter. He had taken Baroney to lunch. She wanted to go to the Ritz . "I was afraid she might make a scene, come on like Bankhead, waving a cigarette holder and making demands in a loud voice. The room is so large and bright, the tumblers so blue, the waiters so impeccable, the hush so pervasive—like a surgeon's waiting room. You have to talk in a low voice or people at the next table will hear you. But she behaved herself, even wore a suit and a frilly blouse." Baroney obviously hadn't been wooed in quite some time and toyed with Charlie who, when he tried out the ghost idea, was surprised by her vehemence. "'I can do my own writing thank you very much.' Then she said, 'How much?' I nearly choked on my scrod. "You mean, how much advance are we offering?" 'I'm no dummy,' she'd said. 'Maybe I haven't made a movie in twenty years, but I know what goes on.'"

She had a devoted fan club. Her fans wrote her more than a hundred letters a week. Besides, she told Charlie, she had had similar offers from two other publishers. He didn't believe her but had to play along or risk implying that she was a liar. These were just the sort of mind games

Charlie most disliked playing. He preferred to read and edit—with the pesky author nowhere in sight or sound.

After he took her home in a taxi—"Twelve bucks!"—she told him to come back the next day and he'd have his answer.

After getting Charlie's second letter I phoned him and we discussed the project. Should we sweeten the pot, already at a hefty thirty thousand, or should we stick to our original figure and see if she caves?

So we went up fifteen hundred, and Baroney agreed to talk to a ghostwriter who would put the story in order and give it a readable structure while she would do most of the writing. It was a reasonable agreement, given the fact that she could barely write her own name and would be grateful, at the end, for the graceful prose of a professional wordsmith.

CHAPTER 8

Charlie McCann stayed in Boston for three days talking to Lucille Baroney, holding her hand and making her feel desired, sought after. He returned to New York with a promise from her that she would let Griffin publish her memoir. I authorized a raise for him; he was pleased, of course, but said he was only doing his job, a fireman rushing into a burning building to rescue two children and a puppy.

"That's what I'm paid to do," he said. Knowing Charlie, I was sure this wasn't a case of false modesty.

"Let's have lunch to celebrate," I said. We went to Louis XIV and ordered Bombay gin martinis. We toasted each other.

"Don't you feel spoiled by all this?" Charlie said, looking around the restaurant serving overpriced meals to well-heeled customers, most of whom were on expense accounts. "I do. Did I ever tell you my father owned a tavern in Hell's Kitchen? We lived upstairs."

I told him I knew he'd come from the wrong side of the tracks but not about the tavern.

"Prohibition was tough for our family. Nobody mentions that. Those fucking women with their bibles."

I considered the many differences between us, and remembering how when we met at school I was shocked by his trousers, which were dark blue and shiny.

"You've come a long way," I said, then realized that he

134

might take this as condescension. But he didn't react as if I had condescended to him. He just smiled at me.

I realized that Charlie had said something to me, but I hadn't heard a word of it. He was saying, "So, Walt, what's your take?" and I didn't have any idea what he was talking about. This is because a few hours earlier Barry and I had had a tête-à-tête in the car during which he told me he loved me, a sentiment he usually avoided as being too explicit, not sufficiently ironic. Nevertheless, it warmed me. It also made me wonder why he was telling me this now. Had something shifted in our relationship? Was something about to change? So I was somewhat distracted not by out-and-out worry but by a knife-edge of anxiety that kept nicking me.

Over an excellent, meal—steak tartare, lobster salad, espresso—Charlie and I talked about the problems we might face in getting Lucille to open up to a writer assigned to ghostwrite her book. Charlie repeated to me that when he brought up the subject of someone else doing the actual putting down of sentences and paragraphs she bristled. "I don't need a writer. I'm the writer."

"No darling, you're the actress," Charlie told her.

He assured her that the hired writer would only ask her questions designed to trigger long-buried memories. She should not mind some editing; every writer needs some editing. "He's going to put words in my mouth," Baroney had said. "I don't want that. You think I can't think for myself? That my memory's shot?" Charlie said she got hot under the collar. He plied her with strong spirits; her preferred drink was single malt whiskey. "Natch," Charlie said. She calmed down enough to let herself be persuaded that the hired writer would not interfere with her thought processes in any way. "It was the liquor what done it," Charlie told me. "For an actress she's pretty sharp."

I thanked him again; he asked me to stop thanking

135

him and changed the subject with a rather heavy hand, but that was all right; I was beginning to tire of it myself. He wanted to know more about Phyllis' boss' suicide. He'd read about it in the newspapers, heard it discussed on the radio and television, but was there more? Had Arnie been depressed?

Charlie seemed absorbed in the details of Arnie's suicide. He didn't know Phyllis well although he and his wife Marian had been to dinner at our house several times. So he knew her mainly as his hostess, a role she sparkled in. Bette Davis at the dinner table. Sometimes when I watched her charming the man to her right, then the man to her left, I wondered how I could ever have been drawn to her.

Charlie furrowed his brow. How much did I know about Arnie? Did he leave a note? Did he open the window before he jumped? Had he said anything at breakfast that would have led his wife to prick up her ears? Did I think he had been unfairly accused? He switched gears: How would I like to spend the rest of my life in Costa Rica? He'd heard that life there was easy, simple and straightforward, no one on your ass, trying to make you look like a criminal.

"What are you talking about?" I said.

"Just idle speculation. I'm fed up to here with this fucking government. It can't happen here? Man, it's happening right now. Arnie had to be clinically depressed."

"Either that or he was faced with a choice he didn't want to make. So whoosh—out the window!"

For the first time I could remember, Charlie looked at me as if he didn't like me.

"Sorry," I said. "It's no joke, I know."

"That's okay," he said, looking at his watch. "Let's get back, there's a week's worth of work on my desk. Thanks for lunch."

We walked back to the office, using small talk to cover over the small fissure that had somehow opened up between us during lunch. I had absolutely no clue as to what had set Charlie off. Was it Madame Baroney and her ego? Or the nature of his job, which clearly was changing from painstaking literary mining and accumulation into something much more like the naked commerce of sparkling merchandise—beads and trinkets? Who knew? Maybe his wife had woken up on the wrong side of the bed and chewed him out for not carrying his breakfast things over to the sink.

"MISTER SAMSON?" Mid-morning on a Saturday the shiny face of the cook preceded her body into my study. For a change, I was concentrating solely on the work in front of me, undistracted by problems domestic or otherwise, not by Phyllis, Kate, or even Barry, who for the past several days had been especially cheerful and seemingly content with his living arrangements. To emphasize its permanence he had bought a ficus plant and installed it in his room, watering it religiously, and watching it grow as if it were a child.

"Come in, Grete," I said, suppressing a gesture of annoyance.

"May I come in, sir?" she said.

"I just told you to come in," I said.

"Thank you sir," she said. She had on her cook's uniform, white dress, white apron with dark marks of grease I figured couldn't be laundered out, white shoes with laces. Her hair was pulled tightly over her scalp and fixed in back in a bun. It occurred to me that I hadn't the slightest idea where this woman came from. She had an indeterminate accent. Middle Europe? A little east of that? She looked to be in her late forties or early fifties. I didn't know anything about her except her cooking. She probably wasn't married because she lived upstairs in my house. But did she have a beau? What did she do on her days off? I couldn't imagine.

Spend the evening dancing the polka in Queens? Meet with her girlfriends at Childs for a meal cooked by someone else? Visit her old mother on Staten Island? Who was she?

Grete hesitated, unused to venturing this far from her kitchen and the back stairs.

I urged her again to come in. This time she stepped over the threshold. She was large, not so much fat as large, her bones thicker than mine. Her shoes were as long as mine. I looked away from her feet, not wanting to embarrass her.

"What can I do for you, Grete?"

"Well I hate to bother you sir, but . . ." She stopped. Her eyes were glistening. "Marie and I were wondering, Mr. Samson, what Mr. Barry's duties are. I don't mean to snitch, sir, but we were wondering why he's always hanging about in the kitchen and his legs getting in the way when I'm trying to mop the floor, and he won't run any errands for me, like down to Gristede's for a head of lettuce."

"None of your business" was on the tip of my tongue, the words scrambling to escape from my mouth, but I clamped my jaws together.

"If you'd like, Grete, I'll speak to him about doing more work around the house and especially about not getting in your way. You know of course, he was hired to drive me and Mrs. Samson in the car. So it's not surprising he seems to have less work to do than let's say, you or Marie." I paused and waited for her to say something more but she kept her own mouth shut. "I'll tell Barry to run your errands for you—although, as I said, that wasn't in his original job description."

"I don't know anything about description but I know about other things," she said.

"What are you driving at, Grete?"

"Nothing, Mr. Samson. I wasn't driving at anything."

"Is there anything else, Grete?"

"Just one more little thing, Mr. Samson. I went to the

eye doctor on Thursday, my day off you know, and he says I need a pair of glasses. I never needed glasses before. All of a sudden my eyes went bad on me and I can't see the little things like I used to." She held up her left hand where a Band-Aid lay across her index finger. "You see? I cut myself slicing the onions, I couldn't see right. First time I've ever done that. I bled like a cut pig, honestly. And last week I couldn't thread the needle. Five minutes I was trying to get the thread through that little hole so I could mend my stockings. I'll need a pair of glasses then, the doctor said so. They cost a lot of money, I think. I was wondering if you could see clear to give me a little raise to help pay for my new spectacles?"

I told Grete I thought that could be arranged. I would talk to Mrs. Samson but I was sure there wouldn't be a problem. She'd been with us for three years; she was a valuable member of the household. I agreed with her that glasses were indeed a necessary item, not something that if you needed you could do without.

"Oh thank you, Mr. Samson. I'm much obliged to you." She gave me an ambiguous smile.

"All right, then, Grete, I should be getting back to work." I looked pointedly at the manuscript on my desk. "By the way, that pot roast last night—you outdid yourself. It was delicious."

"Thank you, Mr. Samson. I try to do my best for you and Mrs. Samson. I'll get back to my own work now." She withdrew, head last.

I was rattled by Grete's visit. Who wouldn't be, under the circumstances? The thing was, in my experience there were no circumstances like mine. The weight of convention, of what was accepted and what not, descended on me and I felt weak. My heart fluttered as if there were a bird imprisoned inside my chest. I broke out in a sweat. I stumbled upstairs. Phyllis was in our bedroom, reading. She asked me what was the matter, was I feeling sick? "You look as if you were about to faint," she said.

I told her I had a touch of heartburn.

"How can you be sure it isn't a heart attack?" she said.

"I just know it isn't. But I'm going to lie down for a few minutes. Have we got anything for heartburn?"

I lay down on our bed and she brought me two antacid tablets that tasted like chalk and told me to chew them. Like most women, Phyllis had the feral instincts of a nurse; it's possible they enjoy seeing men enfeebled.

"Pretty bracelet," I said. "Have I seen it before?"

"Oh this? Kate gave it to me; she bought it out of her allowance. Isn't it nice? I mean it probably cost her all of five dollars, but to me it's valuable because she's my daughter." Then, almost so softly I could hardly hear her she said, "And we almost lost her. . . ."

So I had given Kate a gift and she had given her mother a gift. It had a certain symmetry.

Phyllis said she was going to keep an eye on me, and if I didn't feel better in an hour or so she was going to call the doctor. I wanted to sleep but I was too nervous. Grete had shaken me—"I know about other things." What things? There could only be one thing. And if I was right, what was she going to do about it?

"Phyllis?"

"Yes?"

"Where's Grete from? I mean she isn't American."

"She's from Latvia," Phyllis said. "Why?"

"Oh, I don't know. I guess I feel a little stupid not knowing anything about the people who work for me in this house."

"You know something about Barry, don't you?"

"Grete's not married, right?"

"She was," Phyllis said. "She has a daughter in Chicago. She misses her. They get to see each other about once a year." Phyllis finished whatever it was she had been doing, bustling around, putting away some items, lining up others;

she called it "straightening." She stood over me, a great magenta bird, as I lay on our bed. She crossed her arms. "How are you feeling now?" she said. "Any better?"

"Well, now that you ask, it makes me feel lousy to realize you know all about Grete and I know virtually nothing. I do care about other people."

"I know you do, Walt. Men don't bother about those kinds of things."

"Grete needs glasses," I said. "She asked for a raise."

Phyllis seemed startled by this announcement. "I take care of those things," Phyllis said. "You've never had anything to do with the servants' concerns."

I told her I had no idea why Grete had decided to apply to me rather than to her for a raise. "Maybe she thinks I'm a softer touch."

Phyllis had drawn a light quilt up over me. She was frowning, possibly a sign of concern, probably something else. I asked when Grete had last been given a raise. Phyllis said about a year ago. We agreed she did her work well in spite of making a couple of bad mistakes, like over-roasted turkey and a soufflé that had failed to rise and lay in the bottom of the casserole like a piece of blotting paper. Otherwise, her meals were pretty good (though hardly what James Beard would have awarded a blue ribbon). She was never sick and hadn't, as far as I knew—and up until a few minutes earlier—complained about working conditions in our house or anything else. She didn't filch our booze or stagger into the house after her day off. A quiet, functioning retainer. That I suspected her motives and was frightened by the possibilities this opened up, I had to keep to myself. I had to act as if what I was saying to my wife was what I was really thinking. This was hard work; it's hard work to pull a lie along behind you, it's fucking heavy. I imagine this is what normal men go through when they're messing around with a woman. The only difference was that my lover was a man and he lived in my house, and now my cook was trying to shake me down and I didn't have the balls to tell her to get lost. I didn't have the balls to remove myself, more or less surgically, from a situation that could only get worse. I had lived my romantic fantasy for so long that I had begun to believe that it would never end.

❧

Meanwhile, life at Griffin went on much as before. With Charlie's help, I hired a young man with a Ph.D. in English Literature from Yale to be Mme. Baroney's ghost. She had got herself one of the most prominent literary agents, possessed of shark-like instincts and skills. This woman insisted that Lucille Baroney's name would be the only one on the title page. Fortunately, that was okay with my young scholar who told me that the only reason he was doing this was for the money. His friends, he said, were "aghast" at his assignment. I could have asked him why he chose this demeaning job instead of teaching in some nice clean school like Exeter or New Trier High, but I refrained because I didn't want to hear any more about the lives of people whom I might not ever see again. I was capable of taking in just so much personal information—in the same way I could never go around and study more than four or five rooms of paintings at the Met or any museum, without my eyes beginning to swirl like a Van Gogh landscape. Just so much and then I shut down.

I did have a minimal curiosity about the young man, whose name I sometimes forgot: Ray Brody. About the business of publishing he was green from the toes up (which made it easier for me to maneuver him) and, I suspect, he was one of "us," although I couldn't possibly ask him or try to get him to confess. We were a despised lot; the descriptive "gay" had just begun to circulate. Given enough drink—and only in the company of men like ourselves—

we might act "gay" from time to time, but mainly we were anxious, worried that people would discover our secret and punish us for loving other men. I gave Ray a tiny office and an electric typewriter and an expense account, and sent him off to Somerville to interview his subject. There, I said to myself, that's one problem taken care of. What's next?

I enjoyed my work at Griffin and found I could do it without going through emotional hoops. Maybe this was because I had so much more on my mind that had nothing whatever to do with the job I was being paid for; this was like playing Monopoly. It didn't really matter whether you won or lost. But loving Barry was like walking across a mile-high gorge on a swinging bridge made from ancient vines, like the one in *The Bridge of San Louis Rey*. And everyone knows what happened to that bridge and all who were on it.

When I got home one evening, Phyllis announced that she and Kate were going to spend the weekend with her sister in Connecticut. Just the two of them. Phyllis said she needed to spend some time alone with her daughter with no one else there. What about Henry? Henry, she said, was not a girl. Girls needed their mothers. Whose idea was this?

"I hear you and your mother are going to Aunt Margo's house next weekend."

Kate nodded. Actually I'd looked all over the house and finally found her in her bedroom at the desk, doing homework. I noticed that her blond hair was growing darker. She turned halfway around to halfway face me. "Whose idea was it?"

"I don't know," she said. She seemed annoyed. "Why? What difference does it make? They have a swimming pool."

"I know," I said. Then I put my foot in it. "Don't you want me to come along? I could use a couple of days in the country."

"If Mom wanted you along she would have asked you,"

Kate said. "I don't care either way."

"You're being extremely rude," I told her.

"I'm sorry. I didn't mean to be." Was she wearing the pendant? Yes, she was!

I wondered why I was making a fuss over their trip. I didn't particularly want to go to Connecticut with them. In fact, their being away from home would mean more time for me and Barry. But when I asked how they were going to get to Newtown, I found out they were taking the car; Aunt Margo had a room for Barry over the garage. The unspoken thing lay between us, quietly gnashing its teeth. I wanted badly to ask Kate what exactly she knew and even to try to explain myself. This would be quite a trick. I live with your momma and together we conceived you and Henry, and I also love Barry with a love so ferocious, so mindless, it's hard to breathe. Looking at him when he's unaware of being watched turns me from an ordinary human being with a sophisticated brain and (with the exception of this one small area) good judgment into a lovesick idiot.

Barry said, "I didn't have a choice, boss." He rubbed my head.

I told him to have a good time in the country.

I felt sorry for myself. I was so accustomed to having things go the way I wanted, that when everything seemed to be going the wrong way I didn't know how to handle it. I was home alone except for Henry, who had retreated to his bedroom where he was reading god knows what. Other boys read smutty books, Henry studied college physics textbooks. He was teaching himself Russian. He was one of those kids other children dislike and adults cotton to. Henry and I got along fairly well; minding his own business seemed very important to him. I settled down with the newest Fleming manuscript and soon found myself deep in the world of his characters. It was a love story of sorts, specifically between a retired air force colonel and a nurse with left-leaning ideas. Somehow his writerly skill made them not so much realistic as real. Their intensity was real, they hurt, you hurt. I was annoyed that Fleming could be so persuasive when he really didn't give a damn about most people's feelings. How did he do it?

"Mr. Samson?"

It was Grete again. My heart leapt up, as they say, but not the way the nurse's did when she saw her beau minus his clothes in Fleming's novel.

She was wearing her uniform. Twin crescents of perspiration darkened the cloth under her arms. It wasn't the prettiest sight.

"Come in, Grete. What can I do for you?"

"Will you be here for dinner, Mr. Samson? And Mr. Henry?"

I told her I thought we would both be here but not to bother cooking anything special—some of that excellent ham we had the night before and maybe a small salad.

Was that all? Not by a long shot.

"There's one more thing, sir," she said, striding solidly into the room, and facing me. "It's my daughter in Chicago."

"Yes," I said. "How is she?"

"She's not so good, Mr. Samson. She was getting very tired, like in the morning right after breakfast she'd have to go back to bed. So she went to see her doctor. He found something in her blood. She needs to have it, I can't remember the word she said . . ."

"Monitored?"

"That's it. That's the word. It means she has to go to his office once a month. It's very expensive." She stood there, solid as a Maillol statue. I didn't ask her to sit down because I knew she would refuse. Grete had the upper hand, but she was still the dutiful servant.

Her eyes bulged and glistened with tears. She took a handkerchief from the pocket over her left breast and patted her eyes. "She can't afford it, Mr. Samson. She's got two little babies and her husband run out on her last year . . ."

"What would you like me to do?" I said. I had learned a technique from negotiating with agents over the years: you never say straight off what you're willing to pay, you ask them what they want. This small ploy gives you a decided edge, like acing your first serve.

"Well sir, let me see." She closed her eyes briefly, probably doing some lightning-fast calculation. "I think two thousand dollars to pay the doctor for a year, probably."

"Two thousand?"

"That would cover what she needs . . ."

Grete may have been a shakedown artist but she was no actress; the tears for her daughter were genuine. So the truth of all this was somewhere in the middle. Her daughter—whose name I didn't know—was probably sickish, and at the same time Grete was asking me for more than the daughter needed. Life is complicated.

I asked Grete what her daughter's name was. "She's Vera. I named her after my mother, rest her soul."

I had made a mistake. With a name, the daughter had achieved a reality she didn't have before. I shouldn't have asked. I was upset with myself. I told Grete that I would have to speak with Mrs. Samson and, in words all too similar to those of our last exchange, I said that I thought we would be able to help her.

Grete thanked me with an earnestness that betrayed anxiety. I don't suppose she was accustomed to blackmailing an employer and it made her unremarkably nervous. I wondered what she would do if I failed to meet her price? Would she go to Phyllis and tell her about Barry? How would Phyllis react? She might ask for proof or some minimal evidence. Grete would tell Phyllis that she had seen Mr. Samson come out of Barry's room late at night more than once, many times. Phyllis might respond that she didn't believe her and fire Grete for telling lies about Mr. Samson. Or she might say that she was grateful for the bad news and would ask Mr. Samson about this matter, and thank you very much for letting me know what's going on in this house. Or she might simply cut her off during the first few words spoken. "I don't listen to tales out of school."

What did I really want? It was getting to be a nasty habit, this asking myself what I really wanted. Sometimes I saw myself as controlled by a malevolent spirit determined to keep me and free will apart. I felt as if I were half buried in muck, maybe even quicksand, and I was sinking deeper and deeper into the ooze until all you would be able to see of me were a few strands of hair on the top of my scalp. It occurred to me that perhaps, on some level, I wanted Phyllis to find out from someone other than me and then kick me out. And keep Grete, who made such a delicious pot roast, surrounded by glazed carrots and small red potatoes and swimming in a pond of rich brown gravy. We were just over a decade beyond the war when meat had been scarcer than single male civilians, and the taste of juicy meat sat on your tongue like a gift from an angel; you didn't want to swallow, you just wanted to savor it forever.

To realize I was less than brave was nothing new. The status quo was too charming—literally charming. It kept me in a domestic situation that gave me everything I needed—or thought I needed. Who but a fool would want to abandon it? And wasn't I just the coolest cat at work, so smart and smooth, so well-dressed, polite, and willing to bend and compromise, never raising my voice over accidents or errors the way some of my colleagues did, throwing their weight around by screaming and scaring poor Wellesley girls out of their panties. I was considered to be a grown-up, a mensch—though very few of my colleagues would have known what this word meant.

꧁

WE BEGAN to get responses to the bound galleys of the new

Fleming novel we had sent out at considerable expense to so-called opinion-makers and influential friends of the author. They were a publisher's dream. Words like "riveting," "emotionally satisfying," "gripping," "ravishing," "illuminating," and other assorted "ing" adjectives, as well as "incandescent," and several more words that seemed to me to be praising some other book, say *Anna Karenina* or *Madame Bovary*. Well, everyone hopes their prose will land on the book jacket or in some other promotional material. I repeat, a publisher's dream and well worth the money spent on producing the galleys. Fleming was pleased. "Guess I still have the old touch," he said modestly. You couldn't help liking a man who liked himself so much. The Literary Guild liked it too and made it a main selection. Was there no stopping him? Fleming's achievement was comparable to having Cary Grant agree to star in your movie.

So while the walls were developing fault lines at home, things at the office were sturdier than they had been in a long time—although Fleming carried more weight, financially speaking, than most of our other authors put together. Baroney's brainy ghost, Ray Brody, had extracted a plausible narrative—in outline form—from the old lady, and was exuberant about the project. "This is the most fun I've had in ages," he told me over the phone. "And to think I wasted all those years in the academy."

Charlie McCann had settled back in his office editing several "important" books, one about the Cold War, another about racial segregation in public schools, and a novel, slight but appealing, about a soldier based in Germany who falls in love with the daughter of a Nazi. When I brought up the Baroney business he just shrugged and said, "It was a lark."

I told Miss Garter that I was going to lunch and reminded her to make a note of my calls, something she failed to do from time to time. This was serious, possibly grounds for getting herself canned, but I couldn't do it; she was so agreeable in so many ways, never second-guessed me. I figured she'd had a very strict upbringing because she always lowered her head just a little after I asked her to do something, as if I were the parish priest during communion. She dressed accordingly, always a skirt, a blouse buttoned up almost to her chin, and a cardigan sweater; while the secretaries and editorial assistants and the girls in promotion and advertising followed fashions in *Harper's Bazaar* and *Vogue* (copies of which they shared), trying to pick up at discount stores below Thirty-Fourth Street what Bendel's and Bergdorf's sold for much, much more. These girls chattered like birds in an aviary, and focused more on what was on their backs than on a page of type. Phyllis said it was important for them to feel attractive, and to be attractive you must dress in the latest style. I thought this made a certain amount of sense, but I couldn't see wasting so much time on it.

"Are you meeting someone for lunch, Mr. Samson? I haven't made a reservation for you."

I assured her that she hadn't forgotten anything. "I'm eating in my own company today," I said. "A rare treat."

She smiled happily at my lame joke. I wondered if she had ever been tagged by a man.

I took the elevator down to the lobby and crossed Sixth Avenue to Mel's Coffee Shop. No one I knew ate there. I got up on a stool, the round kind with a leather seat that you can spin in a complete circle. I ordered a tuna fish sandwich on rye and a vanilla frappe. The man behind the counter recognized me and called me by name, remarking that he hadn't seen me for a while. I told him it had been a very busy time. When I bit into the sandwich I was almost overcome by the marvelous flavor of mashed fish and mayonnaise, and something sweetly sour. This vacation from fancy meals—sparring with agents over lunches that cost as much as a month's wages for most of the world's population—restored my optimism, and encouraged me to feel that I was up to dealing with the fraught situation that involved Kate and Grete and Barry and Phyllis. I must be crazy, I told myself. What does a man want except a little love, a little peace? I didn't need a headshrinker to tell me that I had devised and constructed my own snake pit. Nobody made me do it, no one set me up, and no one instructed me to follow my less than "normal" impulses. The trick was: could I climb out without hurting myself— and others near and dear?

The man sitting next to me at the counter asked me to pass him the ketchup. He pulled up a corner of the bread of his sandwich, peered under it as if he didn't know what lay there, and poured ketchup over it until it was entirely lost under a running red sea. "You ought to try one of their Westerns," the man said. I told him I thought I would stick to tuna fish. He was wearing jeans and an Eisenhower jacket. I asked him what line of work he was in. "Carpets," he said. "It's a decent living."

"I know," I said. *Just like Barry.* Did Barry have something to do with this? Not just implausible, but impossible. I felt myself growing paranoid. I wanted to get out of there as fast as I could. I paid my check and left. Midtown New York was awash with people hurrying, swarming. To what end?

I instructed myself to quit this adolescent cud-chewing. Maybe I did need a shrink after all. I stopped to look at the display in one of those cramped tourist shops, miniature Statues of Liberty, cheap cameras, Frank Sinatra posters, snow globes, coffee mugs with a picture of the Empire State Building, and much more assorted dreck jammed together, garishly lighted, a flame for the tourist moths who went home and put their gimcrack on the mantel to show they had visited the greatest city in the world. I couldn't imagine living anywhere else. Well, maybe Costa Rica with Barry.

But that was a dream too.

I had a calm-before-the-storm feeling.

WHEN I got back to the office after my solitary lunch, Miss Garter was waiting by the elevator; god only knows how long she had been there.

"Walter"—she had agreed to call me by my first name after almost a decade of working for me—"Walter," she repeated, "Mr. Fleming has called five times. He must speak to you right away, says it's extremely urgent. He sounds very upset. He forgot my name."

"Hold on there," I said. "How bad can it be?"

Even as I tried to tamp down her agitation, I was mentally scrambling through various scenarios. Fleming was leaving the country. Fleming's wife had been killed (god forbid), Fleming had killed someone (god forbid), he wanted more money (god forbid and anyway he had plenty of money; that's not what he wanted). It was rumored that Fleming was in line for a Pulitzer. But then why would he be so upset? I hurried to my desk and dialed his number at home, a number only a few of the privileged possessed.

He answered his phone on the first ring. "It's you," he said. "Where were you? It's nearly three o'clock."

"Having lunch," I said. "Alone. What's this all about? Miss Garter says you've called several times."

"She's right," he said. "I'm extremely upset."

"Okay," I said, "I hear you. What's this all about?"

"It's your editor, Charles McCann. He has to go."

"What do you mean he has to go? What are you talking about?" It occurred to me that either Fleming was drunk or had lost his senses.

"I mean the man's a Communist. Griffin House can't afford to have a man with his past on its staff. This is a serious moment in history, my friend, and you cannot

151

ignore the facts."

I asked him to slow down a little; I was having a hard time following him. "First of all," I said, "he's not a member of anything. And second he's the best editor in the house. He's a fine man, an old friend."

"Harvard! There you go. Call it Pinko U. Harvard doesn't cut any ice with me."

"What do you expect me to do?" I said.

"Fire him."

CHAPTER 9

O ver the years I fielded scores of complaints, bouts of crying, threats, curses, and pleas from my authors. They would start out starry-eyed and giddy, believing that the world would wobble or the sun rise and set twice on the same day, the very day their book was published. Gradually, as the truth sank in, the voice dropped, the eyes brimmed. "You mean you're going to buy only *one* ad?" "You mean you're not going to send me to San Francisco?" Then came the calls asking how many copies of their books had sold. I had one author who called five times a week to check on his sales. Finally I just pulled a number out of the ether and told him that. But I had never heard anything like the complaint lodged by Edgar Fleming.

Maybe, I told myself, Fleming was joking, having a little fun at my expense. I tested my theory. He assured me that he was not joking and accused me of making light of an extremely serious situation. Did I sense a veiled threat that if I didn't get rid of Charlie, Fleming would no longer publish his books with Griffin? There was an unsavory edge to his voice, something I'd heard only once or twice before. "There are a lot of dandy publishers out there," he said.

I suggested he come into the office so we could talk about it. He said, "I'd rather not show up at your office. Why don't you stop by my place after work? No, that's no good, Mary's here and I'd rather there were no distractions. She'd want to put her two cents in."

I asked Fleming if his wife agreed with him about this matter.

"I haven't told her about it." An all-American marriage. I suggested we meet at the Oak Bar. "Too public," he said. "Everybody knows me there—it's distracting."

"Then you say where," I said.

I was anxious to get off the phone so I could talk to Charlie before I saw Fleming. I wanted to ask him straight-out what the story was. The chill felt by everyone in the entertainment and publishing worlds had driven some people crazy—and I mean literally. You don't fire someone for what they once were but no longer are. And, in any case, you don't fire them unless they've done something to deserve it—like cooking the books or screwing the boss' secretary in the mail room (although this did happen and the man was given another chance). Or lying to *The New York Times* about sales figures. Or any number of other derelictions that make you an undesirable member of your community. But because you might have once, long ago, in your callow youth briefly joined the Communist Party? That was bullshit pure and simple.

After agreeing to meet Fleming in a bar on Sixth Avenue, I went down the hall, knocked on Charlie's door, and went in. Charlie was sitting on his couch with a young woman. He looked surprised to see me—although this was hardly the first time I'd done this—and introduced me to the woman. "This is Amanda Benton."

"I think she's going to turn in a terrific book," Charlie said. "Short stories."

He looked at her the way you look at an especially pretty child who might just turn into Shirley Temple.

I apologized for interrupting. Charlie said they were just about finished anyway, but the girl looked surprised. He patted her hand and said, "You go home, honey, and write one or two more stories like the others and you'll have a contract very soon."

After the girl had gathered up her things, Charlie told me he thought she was going to be the next Carson McCullers. "Lots of emotional disorder in her stories, lots of blood. Sex. I don't know where she gets it from. She comes from Scarsdale. She went to Vassar for chrissake! What can I do for you?"

I sat down on the place vacated by Miss Benton. It was still warm from her bottom. Charlie raised his eyebrows, probably in lieu of asking "what's up?"

I didn't answer since I was still deciding how best to put it to him, until I realized there was no virtue in beating around the bush, when he said again, "What's up?"

"I just got a call from Ed Fleming," I said. "It had to do with you."

Charlie nodded, as if he knew what this was about.

"He says you used to be a member of the Party. He suggested I let you go." I swallowed, hard. This was a lousy beginning; I was rushing, skipping the small talk, skipping workplace gossip; just trying to get over the hard part. Not sure exactly what words to use, I tried instead to put myself in Charlie's place. It wasn't the best place to be. Sweat formed under my arms and began to trickle down my sides.

"'Let me go'? What kind of pussy language is that? You mean *fire* me."

"That's correct," I said.

"And you told him?"

"I told him nothing. We're meeting later."

"You told him *nothing*?" Charlie got up and went over to the window where he pressed his hands against the frame, arching his back. "You didn't tell him you had no intention of canning me? Why didn't you? Walter, if you don't mind my saying so—and even if you do mind—doesn't that make you some kind of big-time prick?"

Quick, get a hold of this! "I told you, I'm going to meet Fleming this afternoon. He's threatening to leave the house.

155

I'm going to try to talk him out of it. Of course I'm not going to fire you. You don't actually believe I'd do that, do you?"

He looked at me the way my father used to when I had done something terrible, like not saying good morning to my mother when I came down to breakfast. Not a nice look.

I asked him—"just for the record"—if he had been a member of the Party. He told me he had never actually signed on. But he had attended a couple of meetings in 1938. "I thought maybe they'd be a good place to run across someone ravishing, but the girls were hairy," he said.

"Right," I said.

"You know me, Walt, I want to be left alone. That's pretty much it. Can't tolerate too many rules."

Pity entered my soul. Putting myself in his place was difficult enough, mostly because I lacked the imagination to feel what it must be like to be accused of something, with nasty consequences in the offing, that had no bearing on my work, my life today, my domestic relationships—in Charlie's case, two children, a wife, a dog, and a cat. I could think, *Poor Charlie, I'm glad not to be in your shoes*, which makes me sound heartless. But did he know what it was like for me, to have to decide between him and the hottest author in the land?

Probably not.

"Charlie," I said. "I told you about this to let you in on what's going on. Not to scare you or get you to resign. You're by far the best editor here. You're more valuable to me and the house than Fleming."

"Okay," he said. The phone on his desk rang. He went over to answer it, then put his palm over the receiver and said, "I've got to take this call. We'll talk later."

AFTER MEETING with Fleming at the Blue Clover Bar and Grill, I filled Barry in.

"So you couldn't get him to change his mind," Barry said. We were in my study. Since it was a Friday—no school the next day—Kate and Phyllis had gone to see Audrey Hepburn and Gregory Peck in *Roman Holiday* at the local theater, the place where they served you coffee in demitasse cups in the lobby. They were tight these days, mother and daughter, often together after dinner in a kind of conspiratorial diving bell. This made me understandably nervous but also freed up my time.

"He was adamant. You know what that means."

Of course, he did. He had a perfectly adequate vocabulary and I knew he hated it when I patronized him. Why was I saying the wrong things? I was rattled. I had lost my equilibrium. I would keep my mouth shut.

"So what are you going to do?" Barry sat in a chair upholstered in leather with gracefully curved arms. His dark skin and eyes melted into my fantasy of loving him far into the future.

"I'm not sure," I said. "He's giving me till Monday to report back." I sighed, a big one. "If I let Charlie go I keep Fleming. If I keep Fleming I lose Charlie."

"We've been over that. You're spinning your wheels," Barry said. "You're not getting anywhere."

"I know," I said. "I'm going to sleep on it."

He leaned forward in the chair and asked me if I could seriously consider firing Charlie. If we lost Fleming we'd be in bad trouble financially. We might lose other authors. Agents would shun us. I might lose my job.

Barry made a noise that expressed his disgust. It was easy for him to take this position, I told him. He wasn't involved. Bystanders know all the answers. Barry argued that one author wasn't going to make that much difference.

"What the fuck do you know about publishing?" I said. "You only know what I tell you."

He got up, turned away, and left the room in a hurry, leaving me drained and furious with myself for losing my temper. For the briefest moment I saw myself as being led by baleful forces I couldn't hear or see, but they were there—bacteria of the soul. The moment passed, leaving me horrified at what I had just done.

I got up and went after Barry, but he had already hightailed it to his room. The door was closed and I couldn't risk knocking or even calling his name. I went back downstairs to my study where I tried to read a manuscript, until I heard Phyllis and Kate as they came into the house. I waited for almost an hour before I went upstairs to my bedroom, where Phyllis was already asleep, not pretending, as she sometimes did; she was snoring.

I tried to sleep but the decision I had to make refused to let me. I looked at the radium dial on the bedside clock. It was after two. Maybe I slept a little and then woke. I counted the arcs of headlights crossing the ceiling again and again. I heard a man somewhere nearby shout and a woman shout back but I couldn't hear any words, just the sound of their angry voices. Maybe, if we had no words, like dogs and cats, we'd be much better off.

⚜

THE WEEKEND was a trial. I decided to create one of those schematic, practical lists, so that I could see my dilemma in black and white. I wrote on the top of a legal pad: *Keep Charlie, lose Fleming* and way over on the other side *Fire Charlie, keep Fleming*. Under the first entry I wrote *best editor ever*. He was just that. He could go out and beat the bushes for new authors, he had patience, he was a terrific line editor, he was willing to put up with recalcitrant production people and semi-literate publicity girls just out of college. *Pal since college*. This was something I could not overlook. Especially since the college was Harvard, an institution whose graduates considered themselves chosen people, a brotherhood of the elect. *Solidarity with colleague.* I had worked with Charlie for years, I knew his habits of mind, I trusted and relied on him. He was an especially good egg, undertaking tasks like the Baroney book without too much complaining. *Loyalty* accompanied the previous entry. *Statement of principle against witch hunt.* This was the most abstract and had the most urgent strings attached. One of my cousins had lost his job as a director of children's television shows because he had, at the age of twenty-two, flirted briefly with Communism. One day at work, the next out the door; he wasn't even allowed to gather his things and pack them inside a cardboard box. He was currently slicing bread and making sandwiches at an Upper West Side deli. I didn't want to contribute in any way to this sort of lunacy. One might as well punish a man for having big ears. It made that much sense to me. Under the second I wrote: *My discovery, my baby.* This one carried a great deal of weight. My pride was involved. It wasn't quite like having to give one of your children up for adoption but some of the same emotion was involved. How could someone else take over editing Edgar Fleming? *Cash cow for Griffin.* Nicely circumscribed: solely about money. *Loyalty.* I couldn't pretend that my long-time friendship with Fleming and, in one sense, our mutual dependence had fostered a sense of loyalty—at least in me. I was beginning to realize that there wasn't much in him towards me. *Long-time friend.* This notation was similar to Charlie's. Although I had known Charlie longer, I couldn't deny that I was attached to Fleming, which made us perfect *drinking pals.* And our *common experience during the war* bled into my memory of that time with now bittersweet consequences.

When I got to the office the following Monday, there was a note on my desk from Miss Garter saying that Fleming had called and would like me to call him back as soon as I came in.

This message kept me from procrastinating. I took out a cigarette and lit it before I dialed Fleming's number. For a moment I persuaded myself that Fleming would have reconsidered his threat to leave Griffin House.

"Hi Ed," I said. "You called?"

"Yes I did, Walter. I was wondering if you've come to a decision about McCann."

Before I spoke to him I had every intention of trying to talk him out of his position. But when I heard his voice, sharp like a knife that wouldn't hesitate to penetrate to my heart, my sense of righteous revolt took over. Who was he to tell me to throw my oldest friend overboard? What made him think that simply because he wrote books that millions of people wanted to read, he could destroy another man because of a crazy notion? I hate your politics so I'm going to destroy you. The hell with that. I could feel adrenaline warm the back of my neck. Given the opportunity, Charlie wouldn't have picked up a handy gun and killed Hitler with it. He just wasn't that sort of person.

"Ed," I said. "You know how long we've worked together. You know how much I admire you . . ." I had gotten up and gone to the window where something in the building across the street had caught my eye. It was a young woman sitting alone in a room somewhat smaller than mine, running a brush through the most amazing head of dark brown hair. Over and over again she ran the brush, starting at the top of her head, down the length of her hair. I couldn't make out her expression but her body said, *This is the only thing I want to be doing.* The phone on her desk must have rung because she picked up the receiver with one hand and opened her desk drawer and put the brush away with the other, as if the caller could see what she had been doing. "Walter?"

"You know that Griffin House wouldn't be Griffin House if it weren't for you."

160

"What you're saying is not bullshit," Fleming said. "But it's irrelevant. I no longer care to publish with a house that harbors communist sympathizers. It's as simple as that. What's your decision, friend?"

"I'm keeping Charlie," I said. "I'm not going to fire him."

"Then you're as bad as he is," Fleming said.

"Charlie's a good man," I said. "He's the best. In fact, I don't know many people who can match him in rectitude."

"Don't go fancy on me. I know you went to Harvard."

"Look, Ed, this is as hard for me as it is for you." I never thought I would hear myself say something as silly as this, but here I was pleading via sentimentality.

"You've got me wrong, pal. This isn't hard for me. It's people like you with their heads in the sand who don't want to recognize the threat around us. It's not just pinkos in Hollywood, it's a pervasive disregard for the Constitution. I'm not implying that you're not a good American, but we can't, you and I and all the others watching, let these people take over our country."

It was hard for me to square Fleming's paranoia with the man who had displayed, in his novels, sensitivity and compassion. This was another species, as if he had taken some awful potion that transformed him from a dog into a wolf. Had the wolf been there all along? I don't really think so. I couldn't begin to imagine what had sent him so far to the right that we were no longer speaking the same language. There was no point in arguing; it would get me nowhere.

I told Fleming that I was extremely sorry to be losing him to another house, we would just have to find another Fleming—I couldn't resist this little dig. In response he said I should go ahead and try. This was getting to be a pissing contest that I didn't wish to continue. I told him I had to hang up. He barely said goodbye.

After I hung up the phone I found that I was trembling. And this reaction wasn't so much about the money we would surely lose when we lost our favorite author, but that I had said goodbye to a friend to whom I thought I was chained for life. It didn't matter about his ugly opinions, what mattered was friendship. Gone.

I needed to talk to Barry. Rashly, I called home. Marie answered: "Samson residence." I asked her if Barry was there. "No Mister Samson, he's gone to the garage, at least that's what he said when he left the house; he needed to look at something in the car."

I thanked Marie, kicking myself for asking.

I went down the hall to Charlie's office.

"It's done," I said. "I feel like I've chopped off my right hand."

Charlie was tipped back in his chair. His hands were behind his head. Although his feet were still on the floor, he looked relaxed enough to be half asleep. He told me he hadn't been worried. He knew I would do the right thing.

"That's odd," I said. "Because I didn't know myself."

I was determined to make myself feel better about losing Fleming and began to tick off reasons that there might just be a silver lining in my having done "the right thing."

There was something newly disturbing about Fleming, the hardening of his right-leaning opinions, rare in a creative person; and maybe his assumption that he could make the world around him change to his liking, his preference for order over disarray—not your usual mad artist scrambling to make a deal with chaos, misery, disloyalty, distrust. Just as he kept dozens of sharpened pencils waiting for him to use them in coffee mugs on his desk, so he believed ardently in extreme self-discipline. He had been known to publicly lecture younger writers on the virtues of keeping to a daily (and I might say, killing) schedule. "You mean," one of these novices asked him, "you sit at your typewriter for *six hours* a day?"

There was something else eating at me—losing my temper with Barry. It wasn't his fault, he had simply been there when

I was very upset. Of course I took it out on him; there was no one else around to take it out on. He was the last person in the world I wanted to hurt. Or so I told myself.

Charlie told me that Lucille Baroney had called him to say she was enjoying talking to the nice young man whom I'd hired to pry her story loose. He also told me her agent worked in the same office with Fleming's agent. A rather nice symmetry, I figured—maybe she'll come through with a book that would help fill in the huge money hole caused by Fleming's defection.

◌⸙

W<small>HEN</small> I entered the house, Barry was in the downstairs hall. I don't know exactly what he was doing there, but he greeted me formally so he must have thought he was being observed. I still hadn't apologized to him for losing my temper.

I took off my coat and hat and handed them to him. He put them properly in the hall closet. He wouldn't look me in the eye, though my own eyes pleaded with him to forgive me.

"I've asked Mrs. Samson to give me the weekend off," he said. "She said it was okay."

"Oh," I said. He had never asked for more than one day off at a time.

"Yessir," he said. "My cousin Tony's getting married in Jersey. I'm his best man."

"Cousin?" It was the first I had heard of this cousin.

"Yes sir, Mr. Samson, we grew up together. Tony's a chef. He works at 21."

"Well, that's very nice for him—and for you, Barry. Short notice, isn't it?"

"Well no, Mr. Samson, I've known about the wedding for a while now. I guess I forgot to mention it."

"I guess you did. Is Mrs. Samson here?"

"She called to say she would be late for dinner. Not to wait for her."

It was obvious that he wasn't ready to forgive me for my outburst. I thanked him and went up to my bedroom where I stood in the middle of the room, numbed by panic. I should believe everything Barry told me. Then why was I finding this so hard? It wasn't until I brought Barry into my house that I began to doubt. Before that I trusted. I trusted my wife, my children, my associates, my authors (well, that's not quite true, but authors are notoriously cagey and love to fiddle with the truth). I trusted Grete and Marie. I trusted myself. My doubts were pantry moths in the larval stage, crawling in and out of the flour on the shelf, eating their way through packages of rice, sleeping and making love in containers of tapioca and barley. My mother's kitchen seemed to be their asylum; she wept when she had to throw out everything in her pantry and start all over again. And still they came. They laid their minuscule eggs and multiplied. I once asked Grete if we had them and she shook her head. "Only poor people have them," she said. "Cockroaches too. And little ants. Not in a house like this." My doubts grew from tiny pale worms into winged things that circled above your head.

Mostly—but not exclusively—my doubts were about Barry. Perhaps, in spite of myself, I shared the button-down belief of those convinced that homosexuals were unreliable. That if you were homosexual you were open to blackmail; and that if there were homosexuals working in our government this circumstance could easily lead to treason or worse.

And maybe the doubt about Barry's loyalty to me, who paid his salary and gave him board and room and not terribly much work to do, served as an added attraction. No love without some degree of doubt.

The PUBLISHER—whose name will go unremarked by me—
chewed me out for letting Fleming go. But the news didn't
hit the daily papers, thank god. It did, however, make the
trade magazines, *Publishers Weekly* ("Edgar Fleming defects
from long-time publisher") and *Editor & Publisher* ("Best-
selling author Fleming finds new home at Scribner's").
I tried to explain, but hit a wall. The publisher, I should
remind you, who owned fifty-one percent of Griffin, was not
so much interested in books per se, but in the money they
might produce. He told me that one should never let emotions interfere with business. I told him that to fire Charlie
would also constitute "business."

"You can't really be joining this witch hunt?" I said.

The publisher looked down at his manicured fingers. If
he was ashamed, he wouldn't admit it outright, but I saw
a flicker of embarrassment cross his features and he muttered something about my not taking a decision like this
again without consulting him. He was the publisher after
all. There was, between us, that boundary that supposedly
keeps commerce and aesthetics/morality separated from
each other; anyone who has ever encountered it knows
how blurred the line truly is. Do you want to publish an
admiring history of the KKK even if you're sure it will be a
best-seller? Questions that had to do with money came up
all the time and we both knew it. Questions about loyalty
almost never came up; we were both in newish territory.
Still, he was angry to have lost Fleming.

"What about this old movie star Charlie's been nur-
turing? How's that coming along?"

If he expected Lucille Baroney to make up in shekels
what we would surely lose by losing Fleming to Scribner's,
he was much dumber than I thought. Should it turn out
to have wings, it would still be a one-shot deal. The thing
about Fleming was that he went on and on, one after the
other, big fat books, with big fat stories, memorable characters and even—god help us—a semi-spiritual underpinning.

What a rat he turned out to be. The only thing that would stop him was dementia or death.

I told the publisher that I thought we would have a good strong book. "The manuscript has just gone off to the Literary Guild."

"Why not Book of the Month?"

"Are you serious?"

PHYLLIS HAD not been especially interested in the Fleming flap. She had grown quieter and less theatrical. It was odd how little feeling—either positive or negative—I could muster when it came to Phyllis. I suppose this was because I had by now so little emotion invested in her that nothing she did really irritated me, nothing really pleased me. She might have been invisible.

Lucille Baroney's agent began to make demands. I figured this was inevitable. Lula's I.Q. may not have been as high as Einstein's, but her business sense was finely attuned to what would please the great audience out there. Charlie and Griffin had given her future a reprieve. Her agent, a woman of considerable stature—she was almost six feet tall and rumored to be an illegitimate child of a British Royal—abetted Lula's interests with passion. We gave her more secondary rights than was prudent, we guaranteed a larger advertising and promotion budget than we ought to have, we hired an outside publicity person to shepherd the old lady to radio and television stations, to forums and panel discussions, and lo and behold—we had another best-seller. Charlie said he felt two ways about its success. It was "kind of crummy," he insisted. "Who cares how long Errol Flynn's dick is? It makes me squirm. Maybe I'm just an old-fashioned guy, but I prefer Virginia Woolf."

"You're getting stubborn," I said.

He admitted as much. Then he thanked me again for not firing him. He made me sound like a Cold War hero. I wasn't. I think I did what most men would do under the circumstances. People were seeing villains everywhere. A week or so earlier a celebrated author left his long-time publisher because it had been bought out by Time Incorporated, thought by him to be an evil tool in a polluting commercial environment. We all said this was crazy.

In spite of Baroney's unexpected triumph as "memoirist" and a raise all around for those in management at Griffin, a melancholy had landed on my shoulders. I could feel it as a soft, substantial weight. When I looked in the mirror I saw more gray on my head than brown. I saw lines on my skin I had never noticed before.

꿎

THE FIFTIES were leaving. Henry was a freshman at M.I.T. Kate, still in high school, had discovered a group of girls to whom she attached herself with enthusiasm. One of the popular elite, she was almost never home on weekends. She was reluctant to do her homework, and although she spent many hours holed up with her mother, rarely spoke to me. Our shared secret had not brought us closer but rather the opposite; she gave me the cold shoulder.

The only place I felt warm was when I was with Barry. He listened to me; I listened to him. I loved the way his face changed whenever he saw me.

"You know how I feel," I said one day while he was driving me to Presbyterian Hospital high up in Manhattan to meet with a celebrated heart doctor. This M.D. wanted to write a book about the possibilities of transplanting human organs from the dead to the living. This seemed more like science fiction than pure science but, from experience, I had learned not to trust my initial reactions to crazy-sounding ideas. Besides, this man had impeccable credentials and

I figured he wasn't about to risk his career by advocating something completely mad. I was willing to go all the way uptown to meet him because I figured his time was tighter than mine. Besides, it didn't hurt to go out in the field once in a while.

Over his shoulder, Barry said, "How *do* you feel, boss?"

"I feel like a very old shirt you can't bring yourself to throw out. You know how you begin to be able to see through it?"

I caught a slice of his face in the rearview mirror; he was smiling indulgently at me.

"That's all my shirts," he said.

I went on to explain that just a few more days or months and the see-through part would disintegrate. You would have to throw the shirt away or turn it over to the rag brigade.

"You have the feeling that something's about to happen that will change your life and maybe mine, don't you?" I was about to answer when the car swerved violently. "Fucking Christ!" he said. "Did you see that?"

I said I hadn't seen anything.

"Man on a bicycle nearly got himself creamed." Barry was shaken. He pulled over to the curb and asked me for a cigarette. "It wasn't my fault."

I told him I didn't believe in omens, but maybe it was time for us both to do something else. I'd get out of publishing, he could fish. We talked briefly of this fantasy. Then I said, "You know how sorry I am about losing my temper the other day. It was inexcusable. Please forgive me."

"Okay," he said. "But don't let it happen again. Don't take your shit out on me. That's not what I'm here for."

What is love? I wanted to ask him this but didn't, I suppose, because a sudden reticence came over me. We had enough love between us not to have to analyze it. *Leave it at that. Life with Barry is going to be a continuous question mark. Play it by ear. That's all you can expect.*

CHAPTER 10

Once, years ago, I had promised myself never to sink into self-pity, mainly because, in seeing it in other people, I was moved not so much by pity as by their attempts to make you feel even worse than they did. My promise echoed inside my head but, as it turned out, my determination to be stoic was nothing compared to my ability to feel sorry for myself. I had a Ph.D. in self-pity. For a while after everything exploded, I wallowed in it, perspired with it, smelled it, hated it, drove Barry crazy with it. Finally, it was Barry who gave me an ultimatum: either pull yourself together or I'm leaving.

From time to time I wondered, when disaster strikes, whether you feel worse if you brought the disaster on yourself or if it hits accidentally like an earthquake. And sometimes—and this bothers me a lot—I have to remind myself that what happened to my marriage was not a disaster at all but rather a change so complete that I felt as if I had left Walter behind and was someone else; someone called, say, Robert or Thomas who wears a size eleven shoe—not nine-and-a-half as Walter did, and has a lot of hair where Walter was going bald, and liked for the first time the sharp smell of Florida Water.

After a while the climate grew more moderate, even though I never—that is, almost never—saw my daughter Kate, on whom I had poured so much of my love and who turned me away from her with one withering remark: "You weren't man enough to tell Mom. I'm not even sure you *are* a man."

"They despise us because of the way we have sex? How can that be, boss? Why do they care where we stick it?"

I couldn't answer. I had no answer. It seemed such a minor thing, after all, how one gets one's pleasure. Why don't they despise drunks, who do a hell of a lot more harm than we do?

I thought I would lose my job; I didn't. But I lost a lot of friends and some members of my extended family, who were embarrassed by me.

It all started one evening in early June when Phyllis, who had arrived home before me, was in the front hall waiting for me.

She didn't beat around the bush. "There's a reporter from the *Trib* who's apparently been calling here all afternoon," she said. "He wants to talk to you."

"What does he want?"

She told me again that he wanted to talk to me. "Yes I know, but what about?"

"I should think you would have a pretty good idea." She handed me a piece of paper with the reporter's phone number on it.

"Let him call back," I said. All the while I was looking around for Barry who usually was there to take my coat and hat and stow them in the closet.

"Care for a drink?" I asked. I felt light-headed. It was like hearing that yes, that little scabrous thing on your arm *is* cancer.

Phyllis treated me to one of her more engaging smiles. "Don't care if I do," she said. "How about in your study?"

We went in and sat down on the leather couch. She asked me if I'd had a good day. As a matter of fact, I told her, quite a good day. Someone on the coast had called to inquire about the rights to Lula's story. "Movie within a movie," I said. They talked names: Bette Davis, Joan Crawford, Barbara Stanwyck. The money hanging like juicy fruit off this tree would go on for a while.

"I'll get some ice," Phyllis said. "There's none in the bucket. That girl doesn't learn."

The phone rang while Phyllis was out of the room. I picked up; the man on the other end identified himself as a reporter with the *Herald Tribune*. He was exceedingly polite and called me "sir," and while asking me a series of invasive questions, kept apologizing for only doing what his editor had told him to do. "Is it true, sir, that a Mr. Barry Rogers, who works for you as a chauffeur and cook, is, let's say, in a special relationship with you?"

I told him it wasn't exactly his business. And Mr. Rogers did drive our car, but we had a cook, a Mrs. Grete Solvena—he might want to speak with her about the cooking. I asked him where he had picked up this gossip. He was adamant about not revealing his sources. He assured me he had not one but two, and he had checked the story pretty thoroughly. And was it true that Mr. Barry Rogers had at one time worked for the Winchester Carpet Company?

Phyllis came back carrying the ice bucket. While I talked she set about pouring two inches of Scotch whiskey into two glasses, and using tongs, carefully placed four cubes of ice into each glass. I couldn't help admiring the grace of her hands as she moved through this simple task. Her nails were pale, gilded with a sort of nacreous pink. How I wished that I loved her as much as I admired her.

"Then you're not denying that you and Mr. Rogers are in an intimate relationship?"

"As I told you before, I don't think that my private life is any of your business. If your editor insists on publishing a story about me, I will, I assure you, bring a lawsuit against your paper that will not be in your best interests. Lawsuits are very costly, as you know. Also, very time-consuming. They use up the good services of lawyers who might be doing much more interesting work." I was bluffing, of course—you have to.

The reporter actually apologized for having to put these questions to me. Was he embarrassed by homosexuality? I was aware of how difficult this must be for him, and at the same time I began the process of grieving for an existence that I had known for a long time didn't have a chance of maintaining itself.

"Who was that on the phone?" Phyllis asked, handing me the drink. She stood facing me.

"It was the reporter who called earlier."

Phyllis asked me what he wanted.

This was the moment I had been dreading for the last five years. I jumped over the edge of the cliff.

"He wanted to know if Barry and I were having an intimate relationship." As I said this the blood rushed from my head and I felt giddy; maybe I blacked out for a second, because I suddenly felt Phyllis' hand on my arm. "Maybe you better sit down, Walt."

She wanted to know what I had told the reporter.

"I told him to get lost or he'd have a whopping lawsuit on his hands."

"Walter."

"What, Phyll?"

"That isn't the way it goes, is it?"

What followed was undoubtedly the most searching and, I have to admit it, moving conversation I had ever had with my wife. Why couldn't I love her the way she deserved to be loved? Because of some minuscule malfunction of my heart or spirit. When I touched Barry's hand my own hand ignited. When I touched Phyllis it was if my fingers had met paper, not living flesh. Could I have changed this if, as some people theorized, I *really and truly* wanted to? I don't think so. I don't think so. It would have been so much easier to disengage from Phyllis had she been a shrew, self-absorbed, a rotten mother, a boozer, a liar. But she hadn't given me any real excuse, and besides, she provided the perfect cover for me and Barry. Who would have imagined, given my job at Griffin House, Phyllis' sturdy pedigree and her noble job? Given Kate and Henry, children raised with obvious care and plenty of money, given our splendid house to which no neighbor had ever had to summon the police for raucous party-giving or for any other reason.

"You know," I said.

"Of course, I know. Do you think I'm some kind of idiot, do I have eyes in my head? Don't I smell it, taste it?"

I asked her when she had found out. She admitted that it had taken her a while, maybe a couple of years, although she had suspected for some time before that. Kate clinched it.

"Kate told you."

Phyllis told me not to blame Kate, she hadn't wanted to reveal her secret. She was torn, Phyllis reported. She loved me very much but didn't want to see her mother hurt. What a cruel place to put a child. Phyllis frowned over her drink and dropped her head. I should not have allowed Kate to be so wise. I said it wasn't my doing. I had no idea how Kate found out about Barry and me. Children were smart, sharp, they could smell a rat a mile away.

"How could you do it?"

The conversation, so far, had been on an even keel. Now it was threatening to overturn in high seas.

"Do what? Do you mean Barry or do you mean Kate?"

"I mean Kate. I suppose you couldn't help what you did with Barry. He's a sneaky bastard and he's a pretty good actor. You, on the other hand, have a lot to learn on that score. You're a lousy actor. Your eyes."

I had thought I was fooling her, when all along she was fooling me. I felt brainless. I felt like weeping over my own stupidity. I asked her why she hadn't confronted me as soon as Kate proved her suspicions were valid. An unfamiliar smile crossed her face, a cat-swallowed-the-canary smile, and told me that she figured that so long as the Samsons were perceived as a solid family, she was willing to put up with the man on the third floor.

"Besides," she said, and the smile grew and took on an ambiguous edge. "I had my own friends. Not all at once of course, one at a time. Where do you suppose I got this bracelet?" She stuck her wrist in front of my face. "Did you really believe Kate gave it to me? Where would Kate get that kind of money? This is a real ruby." She pointed to a small red stone. "And this is an uncut emerald."

"Who gave it to you? Arnie?"

Phyllis nodded. "We had quite a romance," she said. "I don't suppose you noticed how damaged I was by his suicide." She turned her head away.

"I noticed," I said. "But it never occurred to me that he was your lover."

"Why not?" she said. She had a point. It should have occurred to me. Did I actually believe that I was the only one allowed to deceive?

"Is there somebody now? I guess that's a dumb question."

Phyllis nodded. Her eyes were misty, no doubt from thinking about dead Arnie.

"Do I know him?"

"I don't think so," she said. "His name doesn't matter. He's the liaison between the mayor's office and the station. We met a year or so ago."

I didn't want to hear any more, not whether he was married, not what his name was. "Does Kate know him?"

"She's met him. Once."

"I suppose she likes him."

"What are you up to, Walter? What's this all about? You bring a sexual beast to live upstairs in my house, eat my food, drive my car, and you absolutely refuse to apologize. You owe me an apology."

I smiled in spite of myself; I didn't want her to think that I took this lightly. But an apology was something you

174

proffered when you spilled the sugar or ran the car into a wall or failed to show up for a dinner date. You didn't apologize for disloyalty and deception; you blew your brains out or prostrated yourself or tore your hair out. *I'm sorry* didn't have it. "You want me to apologize?" I said.

"To start with," she said. "Then you can pack your bags— and Barry's too. I don't expect he has all that much stuff."

This was going much too fast. An hour earlier we hadn't yet picked up our shovels and now the grave was unearthed, nice and neat, with smooth edges, waiting for the corpse.

I stared at my wife, showing me her sad but determined face, and I began to regret everything. Then it dawned on me that my focus was wrong. She was handing me the perfect excuse to leave without guilt, without feeling that I had wronged her, destroyed her life, thrown her away like an old shoe, set her adrift, and all those other doleful images characterizing wronged women throughout the ages, throughout literature. While not quite strong as an ox, she did have grit; she wasn't going to stand for any insults, not from me or any other male. In her own prickly way, she was quite wonderful, and my ultimate punishment lay in not having the desire to make love to her.

She had given me a set of horns and I deserved them. But I had done to her what she was now doing to me—tit for tat. The emotional symmetry gave me a shot of abstract pleasure.

"If we were in France I could kill your boyfriend and not go to jail for it," I said.

"I can't listen to you anymore. You're acting crazy."

There was nothing more either of us could say at this point. I headed for the door to go in search of Barry when I heard Phyllis say, "And don't bother trying to talk to Kate. She's spending the night at a friend's house. I don't think she's in any mood to talk to you."

CHAPTER 11

For more than a year, Barry and I have been living together. We sleep in the same bed. We plan our meals together, although he does more of the actual cooking than I do—mainly because I'm still unsure of myself when standing at a stove. Barry likes to experiment with new recipes. But he hates anything to do with fish except on the end of a line, and won't let it be cooked in our kitchen because of the smell. So if I want some grilled salmon I have to eat it at lunch, in a restaurant, or at the Orange Club.

I gave Phyllis almost everything, the house, the car— it nearly killed Barry to have to say goodbye to Baby; he actually cried—and a bloated sum of money called alimony. The judge who decided this frowned at me the way you would at a dog who's pooped on the living room rug. Kate is seventeen and a senior in high school; Henry's a junior at M.I.T. My son assures me he'll go on for a Ph.D. in an esoteric branch of physics that I don't begin to understand. If Henry had been younger, Phyllis would no doubt have been awarded custody of him. There is no judge on earth who would have turned him over to a deviant. To tell the truth I never really wanted a house that large— except insofar as it allowed me to bring Barry into it and hide him there.

At work, no one said a word about my unwholesome

176

behavior—at least not to my face. This may have been because I was the boss of everyone there, except the publisher. Or it may have been because they were not only sensitive, but actually liked me, and wanted to give me privacy. Worse things had happened in and around Griffin House. Lives had not only been disrupted, but turned inside out, upside down, a suicide here, a gentle murder there. Truly, a murder: two of the mail room boys had, a few years earlier, dispatched the parents of one of them by feeding them cocktails spiked with strychnine. They were, sorry to say, homosexual. Also abandonment, betrayal, disappearance, embezzlement—the usual array of human behavior that, somehow, failed to astonish you when it was you doing it.

The fact that my wife banished me from our house and that Barry and I were now living together in a converted office building, seemed, after the first week or so, to be neither astonishing nor abnormal. I had performed the role of husband and father to near-perfection—never forgetting my lines, upstaging my partner, or chewing up the carpet—so that I began to believe this was the way things were meant to be. When Barry walked into my office that day in his awful blue pants, carrying clipboard and tape measure, a huge appetite inside me broke loose and ran around like a dog with rabies.

When I wanted to make myself nervous, I wondered what direction my life would have taken if Barry hadn't been assigned to measure my room. Would I have met another man who would have set the beast loose? I'm not at all sure, mainly because until that afternoon I was unaware that I needed anything I didn't already have. Passion? Maybe not, but I loved my work and took away from it moments of genuine pleasure, if not glee. I felt rushes of—dare I call it joy?—after an intricate task was completed, a plan realized, a literary strategy brought to fruition with grace (like a book of poems or tremulous short stories that fewer than a thousand people would ever buy), a passage restructured, a richer meaning uncovered by diligent digging.

Granted, it was not quite on a par with singing a Mozart aria from the stage of the Met, but it had its moments, and I cherished them.

Barry generally refrained from making fun of my occupation, although there were many times when it would have been not only apt, but also would have given us the chance to indulge in doleful hilarity. In spite of the fact that we were more than halfway through the twentieth century, publishing was still stuck in the nineteenth. It was a kind of ad hoc, buckshot, hit-or-miss commercial activity pretending to be a profession for gentlemen and, as Barry noted, "It's a fucking miracle you guys break even." For example, the Griffin sales and publicity departments might just as well have been occupying two separate continents, with the one speaking Aramaic and the other Finnish. With high hopes for large sales figures, an author is scheduled for a book tour. He's flown, first class, to Chicago where Mike Royko has agreed to interview him; and the next day, after Royko's column has appeared, he'll show up at Kroch's bookstore in the Loop where people will flock to see him and ask him to sign copies of his book. But the publicity department has neglected to tell the sales department about the forthcoming interview, and so the bookstore has ordered only three copies of the author's book. Everybody gets angry, especially the author, who takes it out on his editor who's blameless for the fuck-up. Barry wants to know why the publicity department failed to tell the sales people about the author's tour. I explain that since the organization runs by the seat of its pants rather than by a set of sensible rules, important things tend to fall through the cracks. "Everybody assumes the other guy will do it, so it ends up with nobody doing it."

"But," says Barry, "if you're the top editor, shouldn't the buck stop with you?"

"Nobody tells me about the tour either. Remember, I

have five or six authors at once."

I should admit that I ought to be on top of the entire journey of the book from the germ of an idea until it winds up on the remainder table at Doubleday's. "I guess maybe you're right," I tell Barry, "but I can't be everywhere at once. How many balls can I keep in the air?"

But whatever spirit it was that kept publishing from growing up and competing in an adult world, it was this same spirit that allowed the publisher to keep me on in spite of my by-now unsavory reputation as a "pervert." The publisher summoned me to his corner office on the day the *Tribune* piece about me appeared. Unlike the items in the *Daily Mirror* and the *News* ("What top editor at what top publishing outfit has enjoyed a peculiar ménage à trois for the past several years on the Upper East Side of the town?"), the reporter had spelled out the dramatis personae. My name along with Phyllis' and Barry's appeared as participants in "a cozy Grecian trio."

The publisher held the *Tribune* in front of my nose as if he were trying to get me to smell it. "Is it true?" he asked.

I looked down at his shoes, premium leather, orange, polished to a fare-thee-well. I liked them very much. I looked up. "Yes. I suppose it wasn't very smart of me to let it get out this way. But frankly, I didn't know what to do, so I did nothing."

"I was wondering," he said, "just how it did get out? This sort of thing is usually kept under wraps. Top secret. You know." He paused to light a cigarette. I will say this for him—he'd made a point of not putting me at arm's length; he had come around from his desk and was sitting in a Scandinavian-type chair next to mine in the area on the other side of his office used for mini-conferences. It amused me, in a sick sort of way, that so many people seemed to think homosexuality was catching: don't let us work for the government, don't let us into the armed forces, don't let us drill your teeth, and don't, whatever you do, let us teach math to your seventh-grader.

I told him truthfully that I didn't know how the story had managed to burst through the walls of my house. Did it really matter? It pained me, of course, to think it might have been Kate—or even Henry. It could have been Phyllis or Grete or Marie. I didn't care; I didn't want to find out. What would I do with the information once I had it? And now that my secret life was hardly secret any longer, I was grateful, in a way, for its bringing my paralysis to an end. I suppose on some level I was grateful to the person who thought he was punishing me and instead had set me free.

The publisher cleared his throat, a theatrical gesture of the kind bad actors use when they don't know how otherwise to indicate that something serious is about to be communicated. "I've already had a few phone calls this morning advising me to let you go."

"You mean fire me, don't you?" I didn't have to remind him that this was almost an exact replica of what I had faced when Fleming tried to get me to fire Charlie McCann. I decided that I wouldn't beg; if he told me I was through at Griffin House I would simply turn and leave the room, not in a huff, but with unmodified dignity.

"Well, yes," he said, "That was more or less the idea."

"What did you tell these busybodies?"

"I told them I'd get back to them. But, between you and me, I'm not going to do it. You're too valuable here."

In spite of myself I smiled.

"Please, Walter, you can thank me if that makes you feel better, but I don't want you to misunderstand. I don't want you to interpret my keeping you on as approving of the way you've chosen to live your life. I don't know how your wife feels about this—though I could make a fair guess. But I'm not sure I want to know. It's none of my business, you see."

"Your business is business," I said. The warm air of

love for this cold bastard rushed over and around me. The publisher, whom I had always considered ninety-nine percent obstacle and one percent good fellow, had saved my ass. Whether he'd done this because he had principles to uphold or whether he didn't want to lose a crack editor, didn't seem to matter at the moment. Either way was okay with me.

"That is so," he said. It was clear he was uncomfortable with free-floating emotions in the workplace. He picked up the paper again. "I was thinking," he said, poking his finger at the newsprint, "that maybe we ought to go after this young senator who seems to have the presidency in mind, Jack Kennedy. Father was ambassador to the court of St. James'. Rich as Croesus. Made his money off of Scotch whiskey."

I told him Kennedy had already written a book—with Harper's. "His name was on the title page but somebody else wrote it."

"A *Times* man, Arthur Krock," the publisher said. "There's a family connection between the Kennedys and the Canfields. I believe John Kennedy's wife's sister married one of the Canfield boys. But it wouldn't do any harm to try and, well let's say, urge him to try another publisher."

I told the publisher I'd write the senator a letter. I half suspected he had done me another kindness for suggesting I go after this politician with the rich father. He knew the chances of prying him from Harper's were not at all favorable. But I figure he wanted to show me that he still considered me to be his best soldier, a man he would send to the front lines with complete confidence in his bravery and strategic abilities.

⟡

BARRY AND I live in a building on Astor Place in what had once been an architect's studio. It consists of one very large, airy room and a smaller room where we put the bed. The landlord had graciously installed a kitchen so small that both of us couldn't fit inside it at the same time. Because this landlord was a penny pincher—and probably skirted the law—he hadn't converted the men's room so we used what was left over: a public bathroom with two urinals, one stall, one sink, and one shower. And a cold tile floor. We share this bathroom with a painter who looks like Peter Lorre and gives me the creeps, and whose work consists of covering huge canvases with black paint. Occasionally, I pass this man going in or out, or sometimes using the urinals at the same time. We nod to each other, he raises one eyebrow; we never speak.

These odd encounters with the painter serve to underscore the fact that physical change has also altered most of my notions about domesticity, my perceptions about other people's feelings, and those few certainties I once had about the future.

But who, after all, has the luxury of certainty? And if that certainty includes the hour and manner of your death, who would still want it? I, for one, would not.

Funny, but having severely pruned my daily activities and moved in with the love of my life, my days at work seem more fluid, more satisfying. Small things roll off my back more easily, I laugh at Charlie's lame jokes more readily, and the publisher doesn't annoy me the way he once did.

I've lost a little weight, which pleases me, because as I fall deep into middle age Barry's comparative youth becomes ever more apparent.

I guess you could call Barry the wife and me the husband. Still the husband. The other night Barry was making dinner for us—beef stroganoff, which he likes a lot and I tolerate. He had clipped a recipe from *The New York Times* and taped it to the cabinet above the stove. I told him to go easy on the sour cream.

"Why?" he said. "I thought you liked sour cream. Jews like sour cream." He said this with a smile so I would know he was joking.

I reminded him that it was loaded with calories. He assured me I didn't have to worry, and I told him the reason I didn't have to worry was that I watched the calories. I can't help but notice that sometimes we sound like an old married couple, and I remarked how nice it would be if they allowed people like us to get married. We could take turns being the husband.

Barry stopped stirring and said, "Sure, it would be cool if we could divorce our parents or land on the moon. Loosen our ties."

"Just a thought," I said.

"You're getting that way again," Barry said.

"Why do you love me? You do love me?"

"Sure I do, boss," he said. "I love you because you're a very nice father. You must know that. And because you have an adorable ass."

"Okay," I said.

"I also like the way we avoid real trouble, we don't get on each other's nerves. Sometimes when I used to hear you and Mrs. S. in the backseat, I wanted to throw a bucket of cold water on the both of you."

"That's odd," I said, "I thought we were unusually civil to each other.

"Think again. And by the way, did I tell you that I was offered a job?"

"No, you didn't. Who offered you a job?"

"That publicity guy you sometimes have lunch with. You asked me to drive him back to his office a couple of times. Remember?"

"Poynter?"

"That's the one," he said.

"What do you know about publicity?"

"I have ears," Barry said. "Don't worry, boss. If I take the job I promise to come home for dinner every night."

⤳

ONE OF the nicest things that have happened since I started my life over is that Barry has allowed me to read some of his journal. The surprise for me is in finding out that he never did make plans to leave me; it was all in my head. There were times when he was very angry: "The Boss can be as stupid and thoughtless as a mule. He goes on and on about his father who hurt his poor little feelings. His father didn't take the strap to him, like mine did, and didn't drink himself silly every fucking Saturday night. He shouldn't bitch." And: "I'm sick and tired of living in this fucking little room; if I wanted to be stuck in a jail cell I would of committed a crime." But then there are moments like this: "I told the Boss I loved him because he's a good father. Also the ass. And I meant it about being a good father. He loves his kids, he cares about them. I never heard him be really angry with Kate or Henry. He acts like they count for something worthy." When I read this last entry I felt warm all over.

I got a letter today from Kate inviting me to her nineteenth birthday party at the Tavern on the Green. On the invitation she's written, "Bring Barry if you think he'd like to come."

Is my life complete? Yes—at least for a while. After that, who knows? But we live in uncertainty, one breath at a time, I and everyone else in the world. I can't think of anything I can add to the pleasant knowledge that I owe no more debts to unanswered desires.